"I'm a Man, Melinda.
And I Want You.

I've wanted you since that first moment I saw you on Deadwood's main street."

His hand reached her breast and a delicious shiver traveled down her backbone. She mustered all her strength. "I want to be left alone," she declared, striving for a firm tone.

"No, you don't," he said, his lips against her ear.

If only she could escape this room. She was beyond reason now, willing to face the darkness outside—for if she stayed here much longer, if he kissed her like that again . . .

She wrenched herself violently sideways, but he was too quick for her, his arms sliding around her to gather her against him. "Don't be foolish," he said softly. "You can't run out into the night like that. Come to bed, Melinda. You know you want to."

NORA POWERS

taught college-level English while working on her Ph.D. A prolific writer, she is the author of some 500 pieces of children's verse, 58 short stories, 9 novels and various newspaper articles. She has been a published author for the last twenty years and reports, "I don't even recall how I started writing, I was so young."

Dear Reader:

SILHOUETTE DESIRE is an exciting new line of contemporary romances from Silhouette Books. During the past year, many Silhouette readers have written in telling us what other types of stories they'd like to read from Silhouette, and we've kept these comments and suggestions in mind in developing SILHOUETTE DESIRE.

DESIREs feature all of the elements you like to see in a romance, plus a more sensual, provocative story. So if you want to experience all the excitement, passion and joy of falling in love, then SILHOUETTE DESIRE is for you.

I hope you enjoy this book and all the wonderful stories to come from SILHOUETTE DESIRE. I'd appreciate any thoughts you'd like to share with us on new SILHOUETTE DESIRE, and I invite you to write to us at the address below:

Karen Solem
Editor-in-Chief
Silhouette Books
P.O. Box 769
New York, N.Y. 10019

NORA POWERS
Dream Of The West

Silhouette Desire

Published by Silhouette Books New York

America's Publisher of Contemporary Romance

Other Silhouette Books by Nora Powers

Affairs of the Heart
Design for Love
Promise Me Tomorrow

SILHOUETTE BOOKS, a Simon & Schuster Division of
GULF & WESTERN CORPORATION
1230 Avenue of the Americas, New York, N.Y. 10020

ISBN: 0-671-45061-1

First Silhouette Books printing February, 1983

10 9 8 7 6 5 4 3 2 1

America's Publisher of Contemporary Romance

Printed in the U.S.A.

In memory of
Charlie Russell
and the West he loved

Dream Of
The West

1

~~~~~~~~~~~~

Melinda Adams smiled as the rented Camaro purred along the highway. The sun was warm on her bare arms and a pleasant breeze tugged at the rich chestnut hair that she had bound back with a ribbon. Anyone from Clifton College would scarcely recognize her, she thought, pushing her sunglasses up a nose that was too short to be classic and too long to be cute. Five years ago when she'd interviewed for the job teaching at the conservative small college in suburban Chicago, she had felt so young and inexperienced that she had hid her twenty-three years behind a severe suit, heavy glasses, and a hairdo out of the Victorian past. And when, much to her amazement, she had gotten the job, she had been forced, more or less, to keep up her "disguise."

Clifton was almost unbelievably conservative in these days of co-ed dorms and "living-together" arrangments, but it had been close to home and her parents. Melinda's smile faded. They'd been dead three years now, but she still felt the loss keenly.

The road curved and twisted and Melinda slowed the

car. In the distance the deep green of pine blanketed the Black Hills of South Dakota—a beautiful sight. It was unfortunate that the road from Rapid City was lined with garish billboards advertising tourist attractions ranging from live serpents to "black holes." Nor was she quite over the shock of discovering that Rapid City, a small place with a population of only seventy thousand, had more than fifty motels, all neatly marked out on a map given her at the service station when she stopped to fill her tank. Of course, the principal industry of the city was tourism. She had known that. But she had not realized how overwhelming the sight of so many billboards could be. It made Chicago's business section rather drab and almost respectable by comparison.

Melinda smiled. Surely in the hills themselves the scenery would be better protected. After lunch she had stopped at Mt. Rushmore, staring with hundred of others at the awesome rock-hewn heads. But her trip was really just beginning. Now she was going to Deadwood.

The roar of a motor outside her window startled her and half a dozen motorcycle riders swept by, their leather jackets and helmets glittering in the sun. These were not the first bikes she had seen, and she remembered vaguely having heard on the television that there was a motorcycle rally in nearby Sturgis. But cycles held little interest for her. She was going to Deadwood. There she would get a feel for the real West.

Her hand went out automatically to the briefcase on the seat beside her. She had taken the precaution of photostating everything and leaving copies at home, but still she kept a close eye on that case. So much depended on it. Her book, *The Dream of the West,* was going to grow out of those notes. It was going to be a big book, big both in the sense of size/format and of importance, she hoped. The book was the reason for this trip to the West. She meant to visit all the museums and collections she could, to tie together with appropriate reproductions a text that she hoped would become definitive in the field of Western art. She mulled the thesis over in her mind. The heart of the West, she meant to show, was the cowboy. Not the brawny macho man of the movies who live for excitement but the tough, durable, dirty cowhand whose work was often lonely, grim and boring, but who endured privation with loyalty and rough humor. To illustrate this kind of life she meant to use the work of Charlie Russell, the great Montana artist whose work portrayed the cowboy's life in all its everyday realism.

Yes, this was an important book. She already had the go-ahead from one of the art field's major publishers. When the book was finished, she would have achieved two purposes. Killed two birds with one stone, so to speak. Melinda's generous mouth curled into a derisive smile—killed was not an inappropriate word here. That's what she felt like doing to Tom Ryder. The book's first purpose, of course, was to gain her the coveted security of tenure—and a healthy raise in salary. But its publication would also show Tom Ryder, whose painting was nondescript and whose scholarship was nil, that her breakup with him was final.

As she negotiated the curving road, Melinda slipped back into the past. Not long ago she had been readying herself for another visit from Tom, straightening the house that had been a legacy from her parents. He had always come to her there, away from the prying eyes of their colleagues. It was so much more comfortable, he said. Melinda made an angry noise in her throat. It had been comfortable for him, all right. He didn't have to stand the cost of a motel room and, after the first year, she had even cooked dinner for him, flattered by his praise into saving him even the cost of eating out.

Her hands tightened angrily on the wheel. How could

11

she have been blind for so long? The whole thing was easy to see in retrospect. Ryder's kindness, his interest in the plain, rather shy, new assistant professor, could be put in perspective . . . now that she knew what a rat he was. She shook her head. Three years of her life she had given to Ryder. Three years of believing in him, supporting his ego, not admitting—even to herself—that his work was mediocre, amateurish. And, what was even worse, taking every one of his criticisms to heart. Her style, her approach, her subject matter—her whole philosophy of art—had undergone a slow but sure twisting to conform to Tom's opinions, opinions that she now knew to be worthless, based on his own insecurity.

But she was going to change that, was changing it now. This book, the dream of many years that Tom had scoffed at, this book was going to become a reality. She would show Tom Ryder what she thought of him once and for all. Melinda shook her head. It seemed incredible that she had let the man run her life for so long, that she could have been so blind.

Still, perhaps she was being too hard on herself. It wasn't until after her parents' death in the auto accident that her friendship with Ryder had become—ever so slowly—something more than that. She did not quite know how it had happened. She'd been so lonely—her parents gone, her high school friends all involved in their marriages and growing families. And Tom had been there.

Gradually she had leaned more and more upon him; he seemed as lonely and alone as she did. And the afternoon that he had first taken her, she had been flushed with warmth over the praise of her chairman, high on the knowledge that she was doing her job and doing it well. It hadn't taken much to turn their friendly celebration into the beginning of an affair. Melinda grimaced: three bottles of champagne, a few well-practiced lines and an experienced seducer. That was all it had taken.

An unpleasant sound burst from Melinda's lips. Less than a month ago she had made her discovery, quite casually overhearing a conversation in the cafeteria that made a mockery of the three years she had invested in their relationship. For long moments she had stood frozen, willing herself not to believe the news which would shatter the life she had so laboriously built after her parents' death. But with the next words, she knew there was to be no escape from this debasing knowledge. "Yeah," said the student who had first caught her attention with the offhand remark about Tom's love life. "Old Ryder really makes out. He's always sleeping with a couple of his students. You know Denise Franklin? She's one. And Rosemary Purvis."

Melinda had forced her numb legs to move, to carry her to a table. She had even eaten her lunch, her mouth moving automatically while her mind raced like a panic-stricken animal through a maze. But no matter what turn she took the truth was always there. Tom Ryder was a cheat. He had cheated on her. He had cheated on *all* his girl friends. And she was just one of them. She rose rather woodenly from the table and made her way out to her car.

Fortunately, she had no more classes that day. When she reached home, she threw herself on her bed. She lay there for two or three hours, staring at the ceiling, her body completely silent and forgotten while her mind screamed at this knowledge she did not want. Not a tear escaped as she lay there and when at five o'clock she got to her feet and stripped her clothes to take a shower, she had made up her mind. She would not see Tom Ryder again. The quarter would soon be over. She was not teaching in the summer. She would go west, back to the land she remembered with so much pleasure.

She'd been ten the last time she saw the ranch in Montana, the last time she'd visited Gramps. The next summer he'd been dead, the ranch sold, and Lefty his old foreman and cronie gone. Melinda sighed. Those wonderful summers—the Montana sun, the big blue sky and the endless stories that Gramps and Lefty told of old-time cowboys. Real men, Gramps would say, winking at Lefty, not them dummies they showed in the picture show who didn't know a horse's head from his tail end. Yes, Melinda thought, she owed Gramps the idea for her book. And so much more.

Deadwood seemed to be just around the bend and Melinda slowed the car in anticipation. Many long years she'd been waiting to get back to the West. And this was where it started—for her at least—here in Deadwood. She rounded a corner and came upon the town. It was a small place; the business/historic part of the main street extended only three or four blocks.

Melinda almost stopped the car in her surprise. She had been prepared for a sight of the old West. Instead she was greeted by a very modern scene. The main street of Deadwood, South Dakota, flanked by historic wood-fronted stores, was filled with parked motorcycles. Not parallel to the curb, but side by side they stood, literally hundreds of them, their chrome gleaming in the sun. It was a breathtaking sight, breathtaking and slightly disquieting.

Disquieting, too, were the crowds on the sidewalks. Men in muddy jeans and big boots, dusty tee shirts and wide leather belts, roamed the streets. Beside them or among them were young women, girls still, wearing the skimpiest of short shorts and halter tops. Melinda shuddered. She hadn't exactly been living in the Dark Ages.

On the other hand, Clifton had never seen the likes of this. A scattering of older people, tourists probably, showed among the bikers, but their presence only heightened the tension Melinda was feeling.

She shook her head. She had no time to consider such feelings now. She had to find the '76 Motel. Thank goodness she had been able to get a reservation. She could check in and then explore the town. She had determined to take her time, she had the whole summer before her. This day in Deadwood would get her started. It was here that some of the West's most intriguing—and lied about—characters had lived and died. Wild Bill Hickok and Calamity Jane, who had been friends in life and made more than that in legend.

Melinda spied the motel and turned into its driveway. She was anxious to get out on the street, eager to see the town she had dreamed about for years.

Half an hour later she paused outside the door to Saloon #10. She knew it was foolish to be so excited. She was like a little kid on Christmas morning, anticipation pounding in her veins. Taking a deep breath, she pushed through the swinging doors. After the sunlight the inside of the saloon was dim. Even so, the polished back bar gleamed, glasses glittering in reflected light. The musty smell of aged wood met her nostrils. Beneath her feet she felt the scuffed planking of the floor. Bemused, Melinda stared at the men bellied up to the bar. With their dusty jeans and boots, they might almost have been old-time cowboys. She shifted her gaze quickly, afraid she might accidentally meet someone's eyes. Her life had been rather sheltered, her immersion in her art absorbing all her adolescent interest, so that she had little previous experience with barroom etiquette. Her only real piece of information was that meeting an unknown man's eyes could be misread as a willingness to become acquainted.

15

And the last thing she needed at this stage of her life was another man.

As she moved gingerly down the center of the long narrow saloon, Melinda had to admit that there was a certain aura of attractiveness about the men, a roughness, a ruggedness. She searched her mind for the right word. A certain virility, she thought, stepping around an empty table to examine a photo of Wild Bill. After all, she was a woman. She was susceptible to virility. It was part of the nature of things. But just because she was susceptible did not mean that she was interested. Men—unless they were museum directors or owners of collections—did not figure in her summer plans.

She studied the old photos on the wall, each properly labeled. The stern old faces, handlebar moustaches and hard eyes gave her a sense of the austere past. Slowly she moved along, making her way to the rear of the saloon. It was not until she had finished with the last photo that she turned to the living picture before her.

A green baize table sat in this narrow space. And around it hunched a group of people, cards in hand. The flash of a diamond on one man's little finger caught her eye and she smiled. They were like a picture out of the past. There was the gambler, his flashy appearance augmented by a dark pencil-thin moustache. She had only to change his tan leisure jacket to a severe black frock coat.

To the gambler's right sat a woman, her mouth a vivid splash of red in the light of the hanging lamp, her lashes heavy with mascara. As Melinda watched, she threw out a card, bracelets jangling on her wrist, scarlet-enamelled nails gleaming. Her blouse hung low on one shoulder. To Melinda's eyes it looked soiled. As did its wearer.

The gambler looked up then and she barely averted her eyes in time. In confusion she swung away. Though common sense told her there were others standing there watching the game, she felt embarrassed.

A light over the entrance caught her attention and she smiled. High above their heads had been built a glass case. And in it, presumably protected from rowdy crowds, stood a simple wooden chair. She didn't need the sign beneath it to inform her that this was the chair in which Wild Bill Hickok had met his death. Shot in the back by Jack McCall during a game very like the one going on behind her.

Melinda shivered. The past seemed all too close here. She moved toward the outdoors and sunshine, pausing only for a moment to throw a last glance at a photo of a grim-faced Calamity Jane.

The sun felt good on her bare arms as she came out through the swinging doors onto the sidewalk. She was very much in the present again as several young women jostled by. One of them wore leather shorts, so short that they were practically indecent. Melinda sighed. That was a world she did not understand: the world of the young who flaunted their sexuality.

She moved off down the sidewalk, keeping her concentration on the store windows. She was probably being silly, she thought. These were people like any others. But there was no denying the electricity she felt in the air, the sense of expectation. Her nerves were on edge, her ears cocked. The sound of a pistol shot, of a brawl, would hardly have startled her. In this town, in this atmosphere, anything could happen. Like it was in the old days, she thought with an inward smile.

The store windows held all kinds of things—from "made in Hong Kong" souvenirs stamped Deadwood, South Dakota, to beautiful jewelry created from rosy-hued Black Hills gold. She paused before a display of Western art. There, reproduced on framed canvas, on

17

posterboard, even on vinyl placemats, were Charlie
Russell paintings of cowboys at work. There was "The
Roundup" and here "Bronc to Breakfast."

The hot sun reflecting off the glass obscured one
painting and she started to shift her position so that she
could see it better. But suddenly the reflection was gone,
that part of the window shaded. She raised her eyes in
surprise and found that she was looking up into a man's
face. He was tall, over six feet, with a strong muscular
build and skin deep-bronzed by the sun, several shades
darker than his unruly blond hair. But his most striking
feature was his eyes, eyes as black as the leather jacket
flung so casually over his shoulder.

Melinda felt the blood rushing to her cheeks. It was
unwise to look into any man's face in a situation so full of
tension. But she could not seem to look away. His
mouth, she saw, was full and sensual; his face rugged and
tough. A powerful man, this one. All her senses told her
so. She waited for him to speak, to make some remark
that she could at least ignore. But he said nothing, just
stood there looking at her, that lithe body held so
gracefully, giving the impression of great power held
lightly in check. Like a great stallion, she thought.

And still he held her gaze, his eyes openly inviting.
Every detail of his body seemed to register on her
senses—the fine bleached hair that contrasted with his
sun-bronzed arms, the dirt-streaked tee shirt that clung to
his chest, the dusty jeans and boots, even the battered
sweat-soaked Stetson perched far back on his head, so
incongruous with the leather biker's jacket. For he was a
biker. She could see that plainly enough. And though her
pulse raced under the invitation of those dark eyes, she
was sensible enough to recognize him for what he was—a
user. A user of women, just like Tom Ryder. Not quite so
subtle in his approach. Not quite so patient. But then, this
man didn't need patience. He didn't want emotional

support or what she had once thought was love. All he wanted was a female body. And right now he liked the look of hers. That much was clear to her. What would it be like—

The shock of the thought brought her sharply to her senses. She was definitely not going to get involved with a man like this. Not with any man for a long time. And never with another user.

With a supreme effort she tore her eyes away and turned sharply on her heel. She was not going to stand there being surveyed like a piece of meat. Her back rigidly erect, she marched off. But not fast enough to be spared the deep rich chuckle of amusement that issued from the man nor his short comment, "Pret-ty."

Her cheeks grew even redder, but she refused to hurry her steps. She refused to let him know that he'd gotten to her. And he'd better not follow her. The stranger, however, did not move. She might have preferred him to, if she had seen the smile of speculation that played about that wide mouth as he watched her move away from him.

When she was sure he didn't intend to follow her, Melinda let out a deep breath. Never had she been so shaken by a man. Everything about him was so blatantly male. A grim smile curved her lips. This stranger made Tom Ryder look like somebody's grandfather.

Well, she would take some consolation from the fact that she was still attractive to men, even young ones. Though now that she stopped to think about it she could tell that the stranger wasn't that young. There had been lines in that sun-bronzed face, lines caused by hard living, no doubt. The sooner she forgot the man, the better. Determinedly she set off for the motel. What she needed was a nice cool shower; this Western heat was more than she was used to.

In the motel Melinda debated with herself. Her encounter with the stranger had been unsettling. She had to admit that. And there was really no need to stay in Deadwood any longer. She could continue on her journey right away. She could always stop here again on her way home.

As the tepid water cascaded over her body, Melinda frowned. She was letting this incident have far too much impact on her. Some stranger on the make, that's all he was. By now he probably had one of those girls out there. There were certainly enough of them and they had no qualms about advertising themselves. Perhaps that was it, she thought. Perhaps because of her blue jeans and her pony tail he had thought her a careless college girl out for adventure. She did look rather younger than her twenty-eight years.

That must be it. She stepped out of the shower and towelled herself vigorously. She had made up her mind. No one, and especially no *man,* was going to run her out of Deadwood. She smiled as she realized how Western her language was becoming. Run her out, indeed!

The grumbling of her stomach reminded her that dinner time was approaching. Searching in her suitcase, she pulled out the lightweight summer suit that she had brought for her more businesslike meetings with museum directors and gallery owners. That was it. She would put on her suit, do her hair in its regular French knot, and no one could possibly mistake her for an irresponsible college girl out for a good time.

Some minutes later Melinda stepped out of the motel with a determined stride. She had even put on her dark-rimmed glasses and now felt herself suitably armored against male advances. What she did not know was that her suit of cream-colored seersucker with its pale orange blouse could not hide the firm roundness of her figure. Nor could the French knot conceal the rich chestnut of her hair. Even the glasses, which she counted on to make her disguise complete, only drew attention to her blue green eyes, now bright with something very like anticipation.

The crowds in the streets had thinned only slightly. Evidently these people intended to enjoy Deadwood for longer. She moved up the opposite side of the street from where she had walked before, but she could not quite keep herself from throwing one glance at that window. Of course, he was not there. A group of middle-aged club women were clustered about the window, enthralled by the display.

Melinda moved slowly on. She was hungry, but she also wanted to see this side of the street. She looked into each restaurant as she passed it, but they all had long lines. Given the events of the afternoon, she did not feel like standing in a line. Finally she found a small place that didn't seem too crowded.

The pert waitress in the Western outfit and boots smiled at her. "Things are real busy tonight," she said. "I can give you a table, but if I get another single I got to ask you to share it." She shook her head. "The boss don't like singles using up all the tables. It's bad for business."

Melinda nodded. She was beginning to tire and she was very definitely hungry. "That's fine with me," she said. "I just want to get something to eat."

She had opened the menu and was scanning its contents when a sudden prickling on the back of her neck made her raise her head. She was just in time to see the man who slid into the booth opposite her—the stranger from the street. For a moment she considered leaving. But she was hungry and the lines were long. Besides that, what was to keep him from following her? She was certainly safe enough here—in a public restaurant. She returned her eyes to her menu. Maybe she could just ignore him, pretend he wasn't there at all.

But the stranger had other ideas. "Good evening," he

said, his voice pleasantly neutral. "I must thank you for sharing your table with me."

She could not very well ignore him when he spoke like that. She glanced up briefly. "It's nothing. Rules of the house."

A slight smile curved his mouth, revealing strong white teeth. "Yes, I know."

Again the blood rushed to Melinda's cheeks. Could he have followed her here, knowing the restaurant's rules? But that seemed awfully far out. Why would he go to so much trouble? A man like this could have any woman he wanted.

"Are you enjoying your visit to Deadwood?" he asked.

Melinda nodded. "Yes." She kept her reply short. She was determined not to unbend with him. Give a man like this an inch—

"I am, too. Though it's a little crowded."

The waitress came then and Melinda gave her order: steak, baked potato, salad.

The stranger smiled. "Make mine the same," he said. "I see you know how to eat, too."

She did not pick up on the "too." He was far too charming.

"Is this your first trip West?"

She shook her head. "No." Her eyes were drawn to the pale golden fuzz that contrasted so sharply with the dark skin of his arms. They were well-muscled arms. And so was his chest. The tight tee shirt revealed every ripple of movement. His hands were interesting, too. Big hands. With long supple fingers. But hardworking. She could see that.

"So you've been West before."

"Yes. But not for a long time."

"Things have changed," he said. "Even out here things change."

In spite of her decision to keep him at arm's length she

couldn't help asking, "What do you mean, even out here?"

He smiled and she felt her body growing warm. "Things change slower in the West. At least in the small towns," he added. "I'm not talking about the preservation societies," he continued. "They work at keeping important old buildings intact. I mean just regular things. Towns like Miles City and Havre, they've still got the same stores, etc., they had twenty, thirty years ago. But they're beginning to get change-minded. These new shopping malls, for instance."

Melinda shook her head. "I remember Havre as a dusty little town."

He glanced at her sharply. "It still is."

When she did not say any more, he picked up the conversation again. "Do you like the rodeo?" he asked.

Melinda shrugged. "I've only seen it on TV." She did not tell him that the only time she'd attended one, she'd been miserably homesick for the ranch for days afterwards.

"It's actually part of the old West, you know."

"How so?" asked Melinda.

"The events grew out of the cowboys' regular working chores. Roping calves, wrestling steers, riding broncs."

Melinda nodded. "Of course."

"If you'd like to see some real action," he said, giving her that warm smile again, "stop at Broadus tomorrow. There's a calf-roping contest there. Team roping. You should enjoy it."

"I won't have time," Melinda said, hoping her face wouldn't give away the lie. "I've got to get on to Helena."

He shrugged and again the muscles of his broad chest rippled. "Too bad. That's the most direct route to Helena. Kind of pretty, if you don't let the prairie overwhelm you. And I'll be there."

"Well, I'm afraid I won't be able to stop. My business is in Helena at the Historical Society." She paused, suddenly aware of what she had given away. Now what had made her do a thing like that?

At that moment the waitress returned with their food and Melinda turned to it thankfully. She hadn't meant to let him know anything about herself. The words had just slipped out.

She gave her full attention to the meal and was pleased to see that he did the same. In spite of the way he had behaved on the street, he did have some manners. They finished the meal in silence.

He did not attempt to take her check, a fact for which she was very grateful. He did, however, follow her outside. The sun was sinking behind the hills and the air was growing cooler. Melinda pulled her jacket around her and turned toward the motel.

"I'll just walk along with you," he said, his hand moving out to take her elbow.

A shiver went over her body the instant that hard brown hand touched her flesh. She jerked her arm away. "That won't be necessary," she said coldly. "I know how to find my room."

Again she heard that deep rich chuckle. "I know that. It's just that things can get a bit rowdy after sundown. This is a Western town, you know." His grin was infectious and she had to bite her lip to keep from grinning back. "It's not the wide open town it once was, of course. But it's still not the safest place for a woman alone."

"I'm quite capable of taking care of myself," she replied firmly.

The stranger sighed, suddenly shifting to a pronounced drawl. "I got to admit that you make it awful hard for a feller to get close to you. But that won't stop 'em from trying."

"I don't see why not." She was determined to remain cool.

The stranger shook his head. "Lady, you don't know much about men. Cowpokes, bikers, it don't matter. They all like a challenge. And in that suit, with that snooty hairdo and those impossible glasses— Lady, you *are* a challenge."

Melinda's first reaction was anger. How dare he talk to her like that? She was about to tell him off when she caught the amusement tugging at the corner of his mouth. He was goading her, she realized suddenly. If he couldn't get her to talk to him any other way, he would goad her into an argument.

Fortunately, by this time they had reached the motel. She turned to face him. "Your reasoning is faulty," she said crisply. "And so is your strategy. I don't intend to spend my time arguing with you. Good night."

She turned her back on him then and made her way through the lobby. She was prepared to have him follow her, prepared to set the management on him. But he did not attempt it. He did not move at all after her goodnight. He only smiled, an amused, superior, strangely haunting smile, the smile of a man who knows more than he is saying.

2

It was late the next morning when Melinda got up. The sun streaming through the window had wakened her earlier, but with a muffled groan she rolled over and turned her back on it. She had tossed for hours the night before, her mind haunted by the face of the stranger who had shared her table. He had been the soul of politeness in the restaurant; there was nothing wrong with his manners there. But his behavior on the street: the frankly appraising eyes that looked her over so casually, the blatant invitation issued by those same eyes when he liked what he saw, and his amused chuckle when she had refused him by turning away—his behavior incensed her. She was not quite sure why. In a certain sense it was nice to be desired. It was not that that had offended her. She frowned, shoving the pillow into a ball. It was the *way* he did, so condescendingly, so—so arrogantly. As though any woman in the world would be glad to have him.

Finally Melinda gave up the vain struggle to get any more sleep and left the bed. As she washed and dressed, as she packed her bag, even as she ate her breakfast and paid her bill, she resolved firmly to leave the memory of that man behind her as she left the town.

Deadwood looked almost deserted in the morning, not a motorcycle to be seen. Evidently the bikers had all returned to Sturgis. Melinda sighed. Too bad she hadn't come a day later, when the town was empty of such disturbing elements. And yet she knew that she did not quite mean that. In spite of her anger, some part of her had enjoyed the encounter with the stranger. She shrugged and turned the car toward the highway. There was no time for thinking about such things. She had work to do. She had to get on with her trip.

The deep green of the Black Hills continued for a while as she wound her way into Wyoming. Melinda did not enjoy their beauty as much as she might have. In spite of all her resolutions, the stranger was not forgotten. He persisted in staying quite vivid in her memory, so vivid, in fact, that when she tried to conjure up an image of Tom Ryder, more or less as an exercise, she found that Tom's features, which had been familiar to her for three years, had grown suddenly hazy, while those of the man she had seen only briefly the night before were etched crystal clear in her memory. She sighed, tucking an escaped tendril of hair back into her ponytail. The man's picture would fade from her mind eventually. It had to. And in the meantime she would get on with her work.

With the car purring along the almost deserted road, Melinda set herself to considering the landscape around her. The road was bumpy, obviously uncared for, up in this little corner of the state where few people lived. She saw no houses, but here and there cattle grazed on unfenced prairie. It pleased her that such open range still existed. Barbed wire had not been able to enclose all of the West.

The country grew flatter, the road more deserted.

Buffalo grass and sagebrush covered the prairie. Melinda knew that the buffalo grass was not what it had once been. In her mind she could see Gramps, sitting on the old rocker on the porch of the ranch house, his dirty Stetson perched on the back of his grizzled head. "Nope, the grass ain't the same. Them honyockers done it in. Them and the sheep. Et it down too close to the ground, the sheep did. But mostly it was them honyockers. Plowed it up and the wind blew the topsoil away." He shook his head. "Shouldn't never of tried to farm this country. This is *cattle* land. Course, can't hardly blame 'em. They didn't know no better. What with them railroad men putting all them ads in the papers back East."

Melinda's foot eased off the gas pedal. Over there, far back off the road, stood the remains of an old wooden shack. Some homesteader's cabin maybe. Or maybe a line shack where the cowboys used to hole up during the winter. She smiled happily. It was good to be here, so good.

As she crossed the line into Montana, Melinda's smile grew larger. This was home, Gramps' home since he'd come West as a little boy of two. She wished it could be hers. Maybe if the book sold well, got good reviews . . . She could look for a teaching job in Montana; there was nothing to hold her in Clifton now. And though Tom Ryder meant nothing to her anymore, it would not be pleasant having to see him every day, having to pretend that they were still friendly colleagues when she really despised the man.

Melinda pulled off the road to consult her map. Her heart thumped a little louder as she looked at it. There it was—Broadus. The place *he* had mentioned. She was not going to the calf-roping contest, of course. She did not consider it at all. But she would have to eat. And she remembered that many towns in Montana were not very

28

large. Just minutes ago she'd driven through a town called Alzada. There had clearly been a sign. But the town seemed to consist of a couple houses, a church, and a run-down bar. Broadus should be bigger than that.

As the car slid along again Melinda drank in the sights. The land stretched away far far into the distance, rolling, almost barren land, only occasionally marked by a small clump of trees. The trees were probably near a creek, she told herself, remembering how Gramps had taught her that if she ever got lost she should look for trees. Where there were trees there was water, he said.

It was getting into the afternoon, and Melinda's stomach was beginning to grumble when she approached the town of Broadus. After the silence and loneliness of the prairie, the little town looked almost crowded. The main street seemed to go past a recreation area where many trailers and cars were parked. Melinda noticed the sign. This was where the calf-roping contest was being held. Her foot slowed on the pedal. She did not intend to go in. *He* would be there. But she was being silly. He would be watching the contest, not looking for her. Besides, she wasn't afraid of any man. Almost automatically the car turned into the parking area.

Getting out, Melinda made her way toward the grandstand area. No one seemed to be charging admission and, being careful to avoid the moving horses, she followed the dirt drive to the fence. This now, was the real West. What there was left of it. The smell of horses hung in the summer air and Melinda sniffed appreciatively. It was a wonderful smell, conjuring up feelings of warmth and comfort, images of home.

That was curious, she knew, since her real home, the one with her parents, had been far far removed from any horses. In fact, her only contact with them after Gramps' death had been at the annual county fair, an event which she had always managed to attend after a great deal of badgering and bargaining with her mother. Her father was a city man who gloried in his business, in the risks and ramifications of making and spending great sums of money. It was her mother who came from the ranch in Montana, her mother who despised life in the West and would cheerfully have forgotten everything to do with it.

But always Melinda had managed to get to the fair. When she'd grown older and had been able to go with her friends, it was the horse barns that held her fascinated. Not the wild rides, or the sideshows, or the carnival foods. Not even those curious creatures "boys," who roamed the fairgrounds, whistling and calling to the girls. Many a time she'd spent the whole day hanging around the horse barns, rubbing velvet soft noses and drinking in the smell and atmosphere of what she thought of as her true home.

Melinda shoved her hands in her jeans pockets and leaned again a convenient tree. Further along the fence horses stood, tails twitching at the ever-present flies, their riders sitting relaxed in the saddle, one leg hooked nonchalantly over the saddle horn. For a moment she wished she had a horse so she could really feel at home. Then she had to laugh at herself. It wasn't things that made a person at home here. It was an attitude. An appreciation for this great land.

Over the loudspeaker came the announcer's voice. "Team 110," he said. The names of the participants were lost on her. Over two hundred participants in this little calf roping contest in a place no one outside of Montana had ever heard of. If she remembered the information on the map, this town only had a population of around 800. She watched the men guide their horses into the chutes. They held them ready, lariats in hands, hats jammed down on their heads. The corral floor, dug up by the hooves of many horses and calves, was a churned mess of mud. Then the gates opened and Melinda held her

breath as the horses thundered out. Ropes whirled. One
went round the calf's horns, another around its back feet,
stretched until it was immobile and the announcer declared the time.

She watched enthralled. It was done in very much the
same way the old-time cowboys must have done it on the
range, rounding up stray calves for branding. For a
moment she blocked out the corral and the spectators,
putting the cowboys out on the range of long ago. A
Charlie Russell painting in real life.

Her mood was shattered, however, when the next pair
of contestants out of the chutes came wearing baseball
caps of white and green mesh. Baseball caps! Melinda
thought. It seemed almost sacrilegious, although a glance
at the muddy earth showed the practicality of such gear.
Better to wear a washable cap than have a treasured
Stetson trampled into the mud.

One of these contestants missed his throw and Melinda, close enough to see the expression on his face,
empathized with his disappointment. "That boy needs
some more work," said a voice near her, a deep voice
that made her start and draw her hands quickly from her
pockets.

Still deep in her empathy with the young man's
disappointment, she heard herself say, "Everyone makes
mistakes now and then."

His broad grin told her instantly that she had done as
he wished. "Hello, there," he said. "Did you have a nice
drive from Deadwood?"

Melinda nodded. "Reasonably nice." She knew she
shouldn't answer the man. But she'd spoken before she
thought; it would look pretty silly to start ignoring him
now.

"Are you enjoying this?" he asked, leaning his broad
shoulders against the tree behind her.

She nodded. Trying to avoid his eyes, she looked

down at the ground. Absently she noted his boots, scuffed, dirty, high-heeled boots, not the ones he'd been wearing in Deadwood.

"Good. There aren't many tourists around here. Broadus is a pretty small place." He looked at her thoughtfully. "Ever been up to the Calgary Stampede? To the big rodeo?"

Melinda shook her head. "No, I never have."

"That's real competition there," he said. "Some of these boys will get there eventually. If they work hard enough."

He was silent for some moments, his eyes intent on the action in the corral. Melinda watched, too, but she could not keep herself from stealing sly sideways glances at him. In profile his face was every bit as rugged and strong as it was full on. His eyes were just as black as she remembered them. Everything about him was as she had remembered it, except that now he wore the outfit of a cowboy—the dusty worn jeans, the faded flannel shirt, the battered Stetson she had noticed in Deadwood. Yes, he looked like a real cowboy, yet she was sure he wasn't.

He turned to her suddenly. "Now, that kid's gonna go far. He's got a way with a rope." He scratched thoughtfully at his ear. "So you haven't been West for a long time."

"That's right."

"Taking a vacation?"

"Not exactly."

His eyes regarded her thoughtfully. "Closemouthed, aren't you?" he asked, his grin taking the sting out of the words.

"Yep."

The laconic Western answer had slipped out unaware and when he broke into hearty laughter she couldn't stop herself from joining him.

"Well," he said moments later. "It's been fun seeing

you again. I'm glad you could make it after all. I've got to go now. My number'll be coming up soon."

"Your number?"

"Yep." His eyes twinkled. "Calf roping is one of my hobbies."

"Are you a rodeo rider?" she asked.

He shook his head. "Nope. Not that good. I just do it for the fun of it." He reached out suddenly to grab her hand, so suddenly that she had no chance to evade him. His hand was hard, calloused, and very warm around hers. "Listen. Wait here, will you? Watch me ride? You'll bring me luck." He grinned. "My name's Cal. You can holler it out if you want. I won't be able to hear a thing 'cept the announcer." He squeezed her hand. "You will wait?"

Melinda nodded. "Yes." The word seemed squeezed out of her throat, squeezed out by the pressure of that warm hand.

"Good. See you later."

Then he went striding away, his lean hips swaying, looking very masculine and virile in those high-heeled boots and worn jeans.

Melinda's heart pounded in her throat. This was ridiculous. She wanted nothing to do with this man. Now why had she promised to watch him? Why? She could not say. But she turned back toward the corral with renewed interest, watching the others with only half an eye, her gaze turning constantly to the chutes from which the next team would come. And then he was there, sitting a great roan stallion. The stallion was excited and restive, but Cal had him under control, his lean body seemingly relaxed in the saddle.

Then the chutes opened and the calf was free. Melinda held her breath as the lariats whirled. Cal was after the calf's horns. In a matter of seconds the loop had settled and drawn tight. His teammate was right behind him. It seemed to Melinda that she hadn't even drawn one breath and the calf was already roped. Oh, he was good, she told herself. He was very good. Could he be a rodeo rider and just be putting her on? She wished she had listened more intently when the announcer had called out the names. But all her concentration had been focused in her eyes. What a grand sight he was sitting the great stallion, so tightly ready and yet at the same time so at ease.

She saw him look at her and wave as he rode his horse out the far gate. Her stomach began to churn violently. She could not stay here. If she waited for him, if she let herself look into those black eyes again, she would be lost. The man's power was tremendous. And now that she knew he wasn't a fake, another drugstore cowboy standing around looking macho, she was even more susceptible to his charm. No, she had to get out of here. And right away.

Hastily she turned back toward the parking lot and the Camaro, hurrying through the gathering people, jostling against some of them as her feelings of panic increased. She was not sure what would happen if she saw him again, but it seemed as though it would be something dreadful.

She had just about reached the car when the sound of a running horse made her turn quickly. The stallion's hooves dug into the ground as he slid to an abrupt halt. In one swift motion Cal swung down, dropping the reins to the ground. "Running out on me?" he said, his forehead wrinkling in a frown. "I thought you said you'd wait." He seemed even taller than before, towering over her.

Melinda's heart pounded in her throat. Her hands longed to reach out and touch him. "I—" She could find no words. He was so terribly attractive. So terribly alive and vital. And she was vulnerable after the loss of Tom. It was only that. Nothing more. "I—I have to get moving."

"I don't believe you," he said flatly, his eyes daring her to disagree. "Listen." The frown vanished. "I'm sorry about yesterday on the street. That was a dumb thing to do. I mean, I can see now that you're a—lady." His voice made the word the greatest of compliments. "I just didn't expect to find anyone like you there." He stopped, obviously realizing that going any further would only hinder his case.

"You thought I was out for a good time," she said.

For a moment she thought he would deny it. He took a step closer; she could smell the faint aroma of soap and leather. "I really am sorry." He smiled suddenly, that charming smile that seemed to affect all her nerve endings. "Will you accept my apology?"

He was so close now that she had to tilt back her head to look up at him. "Yes. I'll accept it." She kept herself from returning the smile. She wasn't so stupid that she couldn't tell a new line when she heard one. "But now I really must go."

"Please." Again his hand captured hers and again she was unable to pull free. "Let me make amends. Let me buy you lunch, a cup of coffee. Something to say I'm sorry."

She couldn't help smiling then. "I've already accepted your apology, Mr.—Cal. Nothing more is necessary."

He grinned rather sheepishly. "But it might be fun. I'm not such a bad guy really. I mean, give me a chance."

Melinda shook her head.

"I promise to be on my best behavior," he said. "I can be civilized, you know. What about last night?"

She had to agree to that. He'd been a perfect gentleman. And she was hungry. Breakfast seemed a long time ago. Besides, what harm could it do? To spend an hour or so with this stranger out here in the middle of nowhere? She would never see him again after this afternoon. Why not have that pleasant hour?

"All right. But I can only spare an hour or so. I've got to get on."

He grinned. "That's okay. I'll take what—" He stopped and pushed at his Stetson. "That'll be fine. We'll go up the road to the restaurant. It doesn't look like much, but they've got the best roast beef sandwiches, and their apple pie is out of this world. Just let me put Red away. Give me ten minutes. And listen . . ." His fingers closed around hers possessively, sending warm vibrations up her arm and through her entire body. "You will wait? No more trying to run out on me?"

She shook her head. "I'll wait. I promise."

"Cross your heart and hope to die."

The childhood words struck some hidden chord and she felt a lump in her throat, but she nodded. "Cross my heart and hope to die. I'll be right here."

"Good. See you in ten minutes."

Melinda spent the ten minutes wondering if she had lost her mind. After all the things she had said to herself, all the warnings she had posted in her mind. Why had she stopped in Broadus in the first place? And why had she fallen for such a line, from a man who could charm the clothes off a store window mannequin, given half a chance. But finally she began to see the humor in the situation. Obviously she had disturbed his ego a little. He must not get many refusals. Not a man like that. Too bad, she thought, that he hadn't gone into the movies. Charm like that was wasted on individual women. He had enough for hundreds and thousands.

She was amusing herself by casting him in various macho Western movies when he returned. "All set," he said. "Red's enjoying a rest in his stall. And now for that roast beef and pie. Shall we take my truck or your car?"

"My car," she said quickly, then felt rather silly. This was not the the kind of man to go around kidnapping women. It was unnecessary for him.

"Great. Nice little car," he said as he slid into the seat beside her. Melinda nodded.

She felt strange going into the restaurant beside him, his hand possessively on her elbow, guiding her. She and Tom had not dined out in the last two years. She was unused to the situation. But Cal was all courtesy. He held her chair, he offered her a menu in case she wanted something besides the roast beef. He asked her what she'd like to drink. He seemed determined to prove how charming and gracious he could be.

The restaurant itself wasn't anything outstanding—a big homey sort of room full of tables and a long counter, the walls decorated with posters announcing coming events and a series of pictures of what were probably the owners, standing proudly with their horses. The place was obviously a family operation. And though it was crowded, the atmosphere was one of comfortable cama-raderie. No one was impatient and the two waitresses looked relaxed and at ease, moving with practiced speed from table to table.

Melinda turned to read the notice posted on the wall beside her—a roping contest to be held next week in a nearby town. She felt herself gradually relaxing as the atmosphere calmed her jangled nerves.

"The place okay?" he asked.

Melinda smiled. "It's nice. Comfortable."

He nodded. "You haven't stopped since you left Deadwood?"

"No."

He grinned. "Too bad you didn't stop in Alzada."

"Alzada? What for?" She asked the question with such genuine bewilderment that he chuckled.

"You did *see* Alzada?"

"What there was of it."

His smile broadened. "The bar's the big stop there."
He glanced at his watch. "It's probably too early now."

"Too early for what?"

"The blackjack game. There's one every night. The
bull riders congregate there." He smiled strangely. "You
might like to see a game in progress. Though I understand the last dealer got his hand broken. Some hasty
patron thought he was palming the cards."

Melinda was not sure whether to believe him or not.
"And was he?"

Cal shrugged. "Who knows? He claimed he wasn't.
The bull rider claimed he was."

"And he broke his hand?"

Cal nodded. "This is the West, remember? Retribution
is swift here. The days of vigilantes are not that far behind
us."

The waitress brought their sandwiches and pie and
they both dug in. The roast beef was delicious and
Melinda smiled. "You have excellent taste in restau-
rants."

"Thank you. You know," he grinned at her quizzically.
"I don't even know your name."

"It's Melinda." She did not offer her last name and he
did not ask for it.

"Thank you, Melinda. I appreciate this chance to
redeem myself." His eyes twinkled at her. "I wouldn't
want to leave you with a bad impression of me."

She returned his grin. She couldn't help herself. "You
won't."

"Good." He turned his attention back to the meal.
"The pie will settle it. You've never tasted pie this good
before. Never."

She finished the last of her sandwich and reached for
her pie. "Now we'll see." She chewed thoughtfully and
carefully. She swallowed while he watched silently. Then

she smiled. "You're right again. The pie is excellent. The crust melts in my mouth."

He beamed. "Great. I'm glad you like it." Then he attacked his own piece.

Minutes later she pushed the empty plate away. "I am stuffed," she moaned.

"Me, too." He leaned back in his chair, perilously she thought. His smile was whimsical.

She was conscious of a deep sense of contentment, something she hadn't really felt since those long-ago days with Gramps.

"If you're not exactly on a vacation, what are you doing out here?" he asked casually.

The comfortable atmosphere had gotten to Melinda and she answered automatically. "I'm writing a book. On the West and its art."

He nodded. "I see. So that's why you're going to Helena." He glanced at her assessingly, then down at his watch. "Too bad we can't talk about it, but I've got to get back. The next round'll be coming up. Will you drop me back at the corral?"

"Sure." Melinda's contentment was replaced by a sharp disappointment. She was very much aware that she did not want to leave this place—or, more accurately, this man. The last hour had been a very good one.

The waitress had a smile and nod for him as he paid the bill. Melinda, waiting to one side, thought how easily he fit into this place. Then his fingers closed around her arm again and warmth crept up it toward her face.

He guided her to the car, waited until she was seated, then closed the door and came around to slide in beside her. "That was good. I enjoyed it."

"Me, too." She saw no harm in admitting that much. Then she concentrated on getting the car out of the parking lot. In only a few minutes they were back at the road that led to the grandstand. "You can pull over here," he said, turning to her. "Thanks for giving me that chance," he said, his hand moving lightly across hers. "I hope your trip is successful."

"It will be." She said the words automatically, overcome as she was by an urgent desire to move into his arms, to forget the book and stay with him.

He slammed the door and came around to her side of the car. "Drive careful now, Melinda. These are lonely roads."

"I know." She couldn't keep her eyes off him. His hair formed a golden halo around his dark face as he bent to her window. She had no warning, no change of expression to signal his intent. One moment he bent there, the blazing sun behind him throwing his face into the shadow, and the next her cheeks were cradled between two calloused palms. Shivers whispered down her back. For one long moment his warm black eyes probed hers and then he said, *"Hasta mañana*, Melinda," and brushed her lips with his.

It was the most fleeting of kisses, yet it made her whole body come alive with expectation. But then he was going, striding off toward the grandstand in those high-heeled boots that looked so right on him. Her heart rose up in her throat and her hands clamped tightly on the steering wheel as she fought to keep from calling after him. He turned once and waved, before he rounded the corner out of her sight, and she responded automatically. Then he was gone. Gone for good. She would not see him again, she told herself. The telling brought a surprisingly sharp, almost physical pain, and for a moment she could do nothing but sit there.

Finally she pulled herself together and realized that the motor was still running. With a grim look of determination she turned the car toward the road. She was being ridiculous to be so much affected by a man. So he was handsome and charming. He was also a user. Any sane woman could see that. She had spent a pleasant hour with him and now she would get on with her life. There was no sense mooning over an utter stranger.

As the car left Broadus behind, she rubbed absently at her lips, lips that still tingled from that brief kiss. She was going to forget him. She was, for sure.

3

~~~~~~~~~~~~~~

It was several days later when Melinda reached Helena. She had stopped to see some collections along the way, revelling in the chance to finally study up close the work of the man she had so long admired. But wherever she stopped she was told the same thing. They were happy to let her see their collections, of course they would give her permission to use reproductions, but for the *real* thing, for the best collections, she simply must get to the Historical Society's Charlie Russell Gallery in Helena and, after that, to the private collection of Colin Marsden, the finest private gathering of Russell's work in the entire country.

Melinda particularly wanted to see the Russell painting recently sold to the Historical Society by the Montana Club. "When the Land Belonged to God" it was called. Specially commissioned by the Club in those long-ago days when Montana's big men smoked, and drank, and conducted business in its sacrosanct rooms, it showed a buffalo herd cresting a Montana butte. She had read that Russell considered it his masterpiece. Reportedly the state had paid $250,000 for it.

She also wanted to see the Club itself, those halls

where women had been forbidden. The triangular brick and stone structure, with a dining room ceiling of gold and a library stocked with first-edition leather bound books. The place where Montana's "big" men had gathered.

There was so much she wanted to see, she told herself, as she swung the car into the motel parking lot. For years she had filled herself with historical information about Montana, read books and magazines, poured over brochures. Now she meant to see it all, all the things she'd wanted to see for so many years. Renew all the dreams she had scrapped because of Tom Ryder's insistence that such interest was "juvenile." The big art publisher didn't think so, she told herself defiantly. Tom Ryder meant less than nothing to her now. A memory out of the past; like a bad dream, he had already begun to fade from her consciousness.

She pulled into a parking space and turned off the key. Yes, Tom Ryder was going to be no problem. She could not quite say the same about that cowboy Cal; the time she had spent with him seemed almost magical. With an exclamation of anger Melinda climbed out of the car and got her luggage. She would forget Cal eventually. She had all of Montana to think about now.

It was several hours before Melinda got to the museum. First she had to stroll around the Last Chance Gulch Pedestrian Mall, gaze at the metal sculpture depicting miners washing gold, amble down Reeder's Alley, the last complete block of historic buildings in the city. The shops and galleries there fascinated her and she stood for a long time watching different craftsmen at their work. Finally she bought herself a hand-tooled leather belt and continued on her way.

At the Historical Society she wandered first through the dioramas showing the seven frontiers of Montana's history, then browsed through Territory Junction, looking with interest at the frontier drugstore and general store. Only then did she approach the Charlie Russell Gallery.

For more than three hours she wandered among the statues, the paintings and drawings, the illustrated letters preserved in glass cases. Every item had to be given its share of time. Though the book was to be primarily about painting, she could not help lingering over the Russell sculptures. The bulging muscles in a horse's neck as it leaned away from the weight of a struggling steer, the expression of determined concentration on the cowboy's face, the perfect reproduction of his workday clothes, down to every last wrinkle—all these gave Melinda great joy. What a wonderful artist the man had been, she thought to herself. Finally, her note pad covered with scribbles, she returned to the motel. The gallery was not going anywhere; she would be back tomorrow.

In her room Melinda plopped on the bed, kicked off her shoes, and sighed. In spite of comfortable shoes, her feet ached. But the rest of her was quite happy. An undercurrent of quiet joy had been with her all afternoon and several times she had almost felt as though Gramps was looking over her shoulder, telling her to notice this or that.

She had felt it most especially when she stood in front of the original of "Men of the Open Range." Here were the lined weatherbeaten faces, the dirty worn clothes of real working cowboys. And the play of sunlight on the flanks of the horses fascinated her. Oh, for a talent like that!

Melinda glanced at her watch and reached for the phone book. There was still time to call the Marsden home and ask for an appointment to see his collection. She understood it had been left him by his father, one of the state's richest men. She sighed. With any luck, Mr.

Marsden would be willing to let her view his treasures, would give her permission to reproduce some of them for her book.

The phone brrrred in her ear, again and again. She was about to hang up when a male voice answered, "The Marsden residence." The voice was so crisp, so very correct, that Melinda had visions of a starched English-style butler. "Mr. Marsden, please."

"May I ask what the call is about?" came the carefully correct tones.

Melinda smiled. "I want to speak to Mr. Marsden about viewing his collection," she said politely.

"Of course. One moment please."

Melinda lay back against the pillows, cradling the phone against her ear. Perhaps her guess had not been far wrong. This Marsden appeared to have servants.

After a moment another male voice spoke. "Jim Pederson here," it said cordially. "Can I help you?"

"I was waiting to speak to Mr. Marsden."

"Mr. Marsden is out at the moment," the voice said smoothly. "I am Jim Pederson, the curator of the collection. Carruthers said you were inquiring about it."

Carruthers! Melinda almost burst into laughter. The name was so butlerlike. She forced herself to be serious. "My name is Melinda Adams. I wanted to ask Mr. Marsden if I may see the collection. I'm putting together a book on the art of Russell. I understand the Marsden Collection is one of the best in the country."

"*The* best," said Mr. Pederson coolly. "Undoubtedly *the* best. So you'd like to see it."

"Yes. I'm building a book around the idea of the cowboy in art. The *real* cowboy," she added. "Of course, I'll also need permission to use some reproductions."

"Of course. I'll attend to that."

"But Mr. Marsden—" she began.

"Mr. Marsden has left these matters entirely in my

hands," the curator explained. "Now, Miss Adams, when will be convenient for you?"

"Tomorrow afternoon? At two?"

"Fine," he replied. "We're in the old section of town. On Ming Street," he continued.

"Very good, Mr. Pederson. I'll see you tomorrow then. At two. And thank you."

"You're quite welcome."

At two o'clock the next afternoon, Melinda drove the red Camaro toward Ming Street. Her map of the city had been easy enough to follow. She parked the car behind a white Mercedes-Benz and got out. Staring up at the huge Victorian mansion, she had to swallow. No wonder Mr. Marsden needed servants. This place was huge. A great veranda stretched along half the front, the other half bulged out in several bays. Toward the back, two great towers, one with a square kind of observation platform on it, the other going up to a pointed dome, reached toward the sky. The rest of the house was equally impressive. It appeared to have three full floors and the whole of the flat roof was surrounded by a wrought-iron railing. There must be a large ballroom on the top floor, Melinda thought, and estimating the number of fireplaces was literally impossible.

She moved up the walk toward the front door, glad that she was wearing her businesslike suit and had pulled her hair back in a chignon. Such a great house was imposing. To have entered it in blue jeans would have been almost sacrilegious. She also discovered that she was quite glad not to have to face the very wealthy Mr. Marsden himself. How could a person actually *live* in such a place? Was that his white Mercedes out front, she wondered as she pushed the bell.

The door was opened by a very dignified butler.

Melinda stifled a nervous giggle. Carruthers was just about as starched and stiff as she had imagined him. "Miss Adams?" he intoned in English accents.

"Yes."

"This way, please."

The entrance hall was just as imposing as the house, but Melinda had only a moment to glimpse its richness before Carruthers was showing her into a kind of drawing room. "Mr. Pederson will be with you shortly," he said crisply.

Melinda nodded. She was hardly aware when the butler left. It looked like the room had been preserved in all its old glory. Certainly wall paneling and furnishings like these weren't made anymore. She almost expected bustled ladies and frock-coated men to enter through the wide doors as they must have so many times in the past. A beautiful old room, Melinda told herself. She wondered if she would see this Mr. Marsden. A man who would preserve such mellow old beauty had her complete respect.

She wandered slowly around the room, drinking in its delights, gently touching a polished mantel that gleamed in the sunlight, carefully stroking a flocked velvet sofa. Finally she sank into a horsehide chair, letting the atmosphere of the room seep into her. She could almost see a fire blazing in the hearth, the room full of gay laughing people, the champagne glittering in their glasses as they toasted their great successes.

No dirty sweaty cowboys here, she thought. Yet she understood that the Marsden fortune had been built on ranching, so some Marsden had once had an acquaintance with dirt and hard work. The present owner, of course, had no need for them.

Then she stopped, enthralled by a painting over the fireplace. It was by no artist she had ever known, a crude

47

amateurish sort of painting, and yet very effective. It somehow captured something of the prairie, of the restless steers and alert cowboys.

"Good day, Miss Adams."

Melinda turned toward the voice. Jim Pederson, she judged, was in his early thirties, a comfortably handsome man. Not striking, but good-looking. "Hello, Mr. Pederson," she replied, taking the hand he offered. "It's good of you to allow me to come."

Pederson shook his head. "Not at all. That's my job. Mr. Marsden hired me to take charge of the collection. It was getting too much for such a busy man."

Melinda nodded. "I see."

"We have made a gallery out of the third floor ballroom," Pederson went on. "It's so large that we can move things around now and then. Also there's plenty of space for extra display areas. If you'll just follow me."

Melinda nodded. She gave the lovely room one last lingering glance as she went out; she would like to keep a picture of it in her memory. So intent was she on getting that last look that her head was still turned as she entered the hall. She was brought to a sudden stop by a sharp voice crying, "Watch out!"

"Oh!" Melinda gasped. The woman glaring at her was a platinum blonde and from the looks of her she was *not* a visitor to the collection. She gave Melinda one condescending stare, then shook her head and, muttering something about stupid tourists, clicked sharply away on her very high heels, clutching her silver mink around her.

"Mrs. Marsden?" asked Melinda, more for something to say than for information.

Pederson shook his head. "Not yet," he replied softly. "That was Nicole Erin, one of the city's richest women. She is more or less Mr. Marsden's fiancée."

More or less, thought Melinda as she followed Pederson to the little elevator with its old grillwork and polished wood. That was a strange way to put it.

"Miss Erin is the daughter of one of the richest men in the city. She gets everything—" Pederson smiled. "And I mean *everything* she wants. It appears that she wants Mr. Marsden. So it's quite likely she will get him. Though probably not for a while." His smile changed somehow. "Mr. Marsden is also quite wealthy. Rather good-looking, too. So I suppose it's a good match."

There was something in his tone that indicated to Melinda that his words did not reveal his true feelings on the matter, but she refrained from asking questions. She was here to write a book and the love lives of Helena's leading citizens were no concern of hers. Though that Nicole Erin looked like a real witch and she found herself pitying any man forced to live with her, especially one with the sensitivity to preserve that lovely old room.

The little elevator whirred softly as it made its way to the third floor and Melinda forgot about Nicole Erin in her admiration of the little machine.

"This was added some years after the house was built," Pederson said, noting her interest. "The house is a historical landmark. We keep it as near its original state as we can."

Melinda spoke without thinking. "It must be rather like living in a museum."

Pederson smiled slightly. "You'd better not let Mr. Marsden hear you say that. Though of course you won't be meeting him." He shook his head. "He loves this old place. Sort of funny, too, the kind of man he is—" He stopped abruptly, as though realizing he was saying too much. "And where are you from, Miss Adams?"

"Chicago," Melinda replied. "I used to vacation in Montana when I was a child. My grandfather had a ranch near Havre. He knew Charlie Russell."

"Ahhh." Pederson nodded. "That explains it. It's really rather rare to have a woman interested in Western art." The elevator wheezed to a stop and the iron grill opened.

"Here we are," said Pederson. "The Marsden Collection."

Melinda stood in a kind of foyer. It, too, was preserved in its former splendor.

"The ballroom is through this door."

Stepping through the door, Melinda almost gasped aloud. The ballroom was gigantic, even with the movable folding screens that filled a great deal of it.

Pederson chuckled. "Yes, it's a good-sized room. Forty by thirty-eight feet."

"Good-sized!" exclaimed Melinda. "Think of the balls they must have had here."

Pederson smiled, his pale blue eyes friendly. "I think you're a romantic, Miss Adams. Most women think first of the task of cleaning such a room."

Melinda laughed. "Not me. I'd be the lady of the house or nothing," she joked. "When we dream of the past, don't we usually put ourselves in an enviable position?"

Pederson considered this. "Yes, I guess we do." He looked around him. "Well, I'd be glad to conduct you personally about the exhibits, but you have that look in your eye of the dedicated art lover, so I suppose you'd rather be left alone."

Melinda detected a little disappointment in his tone. She smiled slightly. "You're right about that. If I could have it, I'd appreciate some time alone. Then maybe later I could talk to you about some of the paintings. Okay?"

"Okay." His eyes were frankly admiring now. "I'll be right over there." He pointed to several desks and some file cabinets unobtrusively tucked away in a corner. "If you need me, just holler."

"I will, Mr. Pederson, I will. And thank you." Melinda fished her notebook from her purse and moved off.

She entirely lost her sense of time as she wandered among the exhibits. Her breath caught in her throat as she stared at a piece of sculpture or a painting, a letter made priceless by Russell's doodles on the border. She stood longest before the paintings that portrayed the cowboy at work. Russell's handling of color, of line, of movement—all of it gave her a feeling of awe.

Melinda was no novice to the art of painting. That was her chosen medium and she had even attempted a few Western scenes herself, done from vivid childhood memories. But they looked exactly like that—childish memories. So she had hidden them away, unable to destroy them because of the emotion that had gone into creating them, yet afraid to let anyone see them. Her mother might perhaps have been able to recall the scenes, but her mother had hated Montana, hated the range, hated everything to do with cowboys. And it had never entered Melinda's mind to show them to her father. For him, painting was a womanish thing to do. He had no time for it, nor for its appreciation. Unless, of course, a painting was worth a great deal of money. Then he might stare at it with a look of bewildered puzzlement, trying to figure out exactly what it was that made it valuable.

And Tom Ryder— Melinda shivered in the warm room. Thank God, she had never shown those paintings to Tom Ryder. In the first unfolding of their emotions she had mentioned the West, mentioned her interest in the cowboy. But Tom had put it aside, subtly at first, but clearly enough later for her to know that he thought this kind of art juvenile. And because she had needed him, she had gradually let the subject slide.

But now— Now she knew she'd been right. There was nothing juvenile about appreciating Western art. And as for maturity, the work of Charlie Russell was just about as mature as it was possible to get. How that man had mastered his medium, making it express whatever he wanted!

From time to time she was aware of Pederson's eyes on her, but he refrained from speaking to her, letting his gaze fall back on his work when she glanced toward him. Several times the muted ring of the phone registered on her awareness, but she was so lost in the sights around her that she gave it little thought.

Late in the afternoon she stood for long minutes before a painting titled "When Branding Comes Round." One of the cowboys was tall and sun bronzed. She could barely see the strands of fair hair protruding from under his Stetson. His hard lean body was all concentration as his rope whirled through the air, just about to settle over the head of a wild calf. The straining muscles seemed to show through the dusty clothes and Melinda had a sharp memory picture of the cowboy Cal leaning in just such a way from his horse, his strong legs gripping the saddle, his arm extended in the air.

She found that she was holding her breath, thinking of that brief exciting kiss. It had been a mistake to stay and watch him, to discover that he was a real working cowboy and not some drugstore copy out to impress the girls. The man in this painting looked so much like him that for a moment it was almost as though she were back in Broadus, the smell of horses and dust strong in her nostrils, the thrill of excitement in the air.

"Miss Adams."

Melinda jumped, startled out of her daydream.

"I'm sorry to bother you," Pederson said cheerfully. "But do you realize that it's five o'clock?"

"It is?" Melinda was surprised. "I'm sorry. I didn't realize."

"We close the collection at five," he said quietly.

"Oh. There's so much I haven't seen yet." Melinda sighed. "I'll never be able to decide what I want to use."

Pederson smiled. "Don't worry about it."

"But I haven't asked you anything. And I have loads of questions."

His smile broadened. "The collection closes at five," he repeated. "That means I'm free. How about having dinner with me?"

He saw her expression of hesitation.

"I assure you I'm quite a responsible man." He smiled. "You see where I work. We can have a pleasant evening together. I'll answer any of your questions. You can come back to the collection whenever you please. There'll be plenty of time to see it all. To savor it."

"That's very kind of you." Melinda tried to gather her scattered thoughts. It was hard coming back to reality after feeling so much a part of the past. The painting before her had evoked the spirit of Cal. So much so that for the briefest second she had almost thought it was he standing beside her. But that was silliness, she told herself. She was never going to see that cowboy again. Pederson was a nice enough fellow and it would be pleasant to have company. She'd been rather lonely the last weeks. "That would be very nice, Mr. Pederson," she replied. "It's kind of you to devote your dinner hour to business."

His smile was almost mischievous. "I don't normally do so, Miss Adams. But I believe this business will be a pleasure. Shall I pick you up at seven?"

Melinda nodded. She scribbled briefly in her notebook and tore out the sheet. "Here's my address.

At five minutes to seven Melinda looked at herself in the mirror and shook her head. She should have turned down Jim Pederson's invitation. It was true she was eager to talk about the paintings, but still, there would be time for that later. Plenty of time. It was really the prospect of a long evening alone, a long evening in which to remember that disturbing cowboy Cal that had tipped the scales in Pederson's favor. This way she would at least have some company. She would not be able to sit around mooning over some man who by now had probably forgotten he'd ever seen her.

She surveyed her reflection critically. The full skirt and soft blouse of pale orange gauze made her look very young. Perhaps she should have stuck to more business-like clothes. But she was getting tired of hiding behind suits and hairdos. She'd just like to relax and be herself. What she needed now more than anything else was a friend. The only trouble with that was that Pederson seemed rather more than friendly. But maybe the man was lonely. Working up there by himself every day, he must have few opportunities to meet women.

She ran a hand over her hair. The chignon had been cooler in the heat of the day, but tonight the weather was quite pleasant and she liked to let her hair hang free. It felt good that way, especially when a little breeze stirred it.

A rap on the door caused her to swing around. "Coming."

Jim Pederson stood there, smiling.

"You're very prompt."

He nodded. "It's one of my virtues." Then he took her arm. "The restaurant here is quite good. Or we can go someplace else."

"It doesn't matter," said Melinda. "I've been too busy to eat here before."

"Very well. Then let's stay. It'll give us longer to talk. And frankly, I'm famished."

Melinda smiled. "Me, too. That brain work is heavy stuff."

The restaurant decor was pleasantly nondistinctive, but the food was excellent. Melinda smiled over her trout, feeling rather comfortable.

"So your interest in Charlie Russell began with your grandfather," Jim Pederson said.

Melinda nodded. "Yes, I used to visit him every summer. Till I was ten. That's when he died." She sighed. "How I loved that ranch. It seemed like heaven to me."

"Too bad you can't live out here. Me, I came out from New York about five years ago. Couldn't bear to go back. There's something about the place that gets to you."

Melinda nodded. "All those years I kept remembering the sky so very blue and the sun always shining. I wanted to ask my mother if I was distorting the memories, but she hated Montana, the ranch, and everything it stood for. She just wanted to forget it."

Tactfully Pederson did not pursue her comment about her mother. "You remembered right," he said. "The sky is always that bright brilliant blue and the sun shines every day. Even when its raining where you are, you can often see the sun shining in the distance."

Melinda laughed. "Chicago's an awfully gray place in comparison."

Pederson nodded. "I know. I spent a couple of years there at the museum. But I like this job better. Except that sometimes it gets lonely."

The look he gave her then was long and rather intimate and Melinda felt a certain unease. She did not want that kind of intimacy. "Can you tell me about the painting I was looking at just before I left?" she asked. "The one called 'When Branding Comes Round'?"

"Of course." His attitude became slightly more formal, as though he sensed her feeling.

"I don't recall ever having seen a reproduction of it," Melinda said. "And I was surprised. I thought I'd studied everything he's done."

Pederson looked properly serious. "That work has never been catalogued. It was done for Mr. Marsden, a birthday gift, I believe. The old man was really crazy about it. Kept it in his bedroom, wouldn't let anyone see it. When he died, the will said it could be added to the collection. But the collection can't be sold, or any part of it, as long as there's a Marsden alive."

Melinda stared at him. "Can't be sold?"

Pederson smiled grimly. "That's it. Can't be sold."

"But—but suppose Mr. Marsden lost his money. That could happen."

Pederson shrugged. "The old man was adamant. No matter what happens to the Marsden fortune, the Marsden Collection can't be sold as long as there's a living Marsden."

"Has Mr. Marsden any relatives?"

Pederson shook his head. "No. He's the only Marsden around. And he's over thirty. If you ask me, he'd better be getting a family started."

Melinda had a quick mental picture of the platinum blonde in the silver mink. "But if Mr. Marsden died, and there was a Mrs. Marsden?" That blonde wouldn't think twice about selling the whole lot. She knew it instinctively.

"Wouldn't matter," said Pederson. "The will is very explicit. If there's no living Marsden, no heir, the whole thing goes to the Historical Society. Intact. No charge. If there was a Mrs. Marsden left, she could keep the collection going, but she couldn't sell it."

Melinda caught her breath. "The Historical Society would need a whole new room to house it."

Pederson sipped his coffee. "For myself I think maybe the old boy had the right idea. When he was young, the present Mr. Marsden had quite a reputation as a playboy. Could be the old man was afraid he'd latch on to some moneysucker who'd drain him of everything. He didn't protect his son very well, but he took awful good care of his collection."

To Melinda this sounded a little unfair. Surely a man with Colin Marsden's advantages could take care of himself. The collection, on the other hand, had no way to defend itself. She liked old Mr. Marsden, she thought. She could thoroughly understand his desire to keep intact the treasures that he had gathered together, treasures that must have reminded him of his youth and his friendship with Charlie Russell. She found that she was very glad that no blonde could destroy the work of years.

The rest of the evening passed pleasantly. And when he delivered her to her motel room door, Jim Pederson contented himself with a smile. "When are you coming to see the collection again?"

Melinda frowned. "I'm not exactly sure. I'm going to the Historical Society tomorrow. Maybe I'd better wait till the next day. If that's all right."

He smiled gently. "Of course it's all right. You don't need an appointment anymore. Come whenever you please. Between nine and five. I'll tell Carruthers to let you in."

"Thank you. And thank you for a pleasant evening."

"I've enjoyed it, too, Melinda. I can call you that, can't I?"

Melinda nodded. It was rather silly to stick to formalities when business demanded she see a lot of this man. "Of course."

"And you will call me Jim?"

She did not like the look in his eyes, but she nodded again. "Right, Jim. So I'll probably see you day after tomorrow. And thanks again."

He took the hand she extended and shook it warmly. Then she was inside the room, closing the door gently. She breathed a sigh of relief. Thank goodness Jim

Pederson was sensitive. If he had attempted to kiss her then, she would not have been at all pleased.

Casually she prepared for bed. Pleasantly tired and relaxed as she was, she should be able to sleep. But the minute her head hit the pillow her mind presented her with a series of bright pictures. She was in Deadwood, staring into the stranger's black eyes. She was at Broadus, watching Cal rope his calf. She was sitting across from him in the little family restaurant. She was peering up at him from the car window, his calloused palms cradling her cheeks, her body quivering as his warm lips brushed her mouth so briefly.

Melinda rolled over abruptly and pounded the pillow into a heap. But her mind did not stop for some time. Over and over, it presented her with such scenes, until she felt destined never, never to forget a certain cowboy's smile or the feel of his lips on hers.

4

~~~~~~~~~~~~~~~~~~

The next morning Melinda was up early. The Montana sunshine pouring through her window might have had something to do with it. But even more important was her resolution not to let that cowboy Cal interfere with her work. She had already let Tom Ryder keep her from doing what she wanted most to do; she did not intend to let another man stand in her way. Especially one she would never see again.

She cleared a table and spread out her notes. Before she went back to the Historical Society and the Marsden Collection she wanted to get some understanding of what she already had. The chapters were rather firmly fixed in her mind. She had poured and poured over all the available catalogues of Russell's work so that even before coming West she had had a good idea of what she wanted to use to defend her thesis. She examined her tentative list. There was time, plenty of time, to examine each picture and determine if it still fit her conception.

One thing she knew for sure. She had to get permission to use that painting that no one had seen before,

"When Branding Comes Round." In fact, she would like to use it on the cover of her book.

She closed her eyes and leaned back in the chair, visualizing the cover. THE DREAM OF THE WEST, it would read. By Melinda Adams. With appropriate credit to the Marsden Collection, of course.

With a smile she opened her eyes and reached for her list and note pad. Today she intended to spend the whole day in the Historical Society rooms. Today she wanted to semifinalize her list from there. Getting permissions to reproduce was a time-consuming chore and she wanted to expedite it. The publisher expected to see copy for the book before classes started in the fall. And Melinda expected to have it ready.

She had allowed herself the whole summer for the job, but she did not think it would take that long. After she left Helena, she intended to stop in the gallery at Great Falls.

And after Great Falls, she wanted to go on to the ranch near Havre. It would not be the same, of course. So many years had gone by since Gramps' death. But perhaps the people living there would not mind letting her walk around a little.

And after that there were more collections. Melinda gathered up the tablet and pen. Yes, she had a long summer's work ahead of her, but it was going to be enjoyable. Every last minute of it.

The day passed quickly. This time Melinda concentrated on the paintings she hoped to use. Taking notes on each, writing some of what she intended each to illustrate. "Bronc to Breakfast" with its bucking horse scattering the breakfast campfire would show the rough humor of the cowboy's life; "Laugh Kills Lonesome," the loneliness; "Herd Quitter" and "When Cows Were Wild," the hard work.

The noon hour arrived and passed, with Melinda too intent to leave the gallery.

It was actually approaching five and her stomach was grumbling indignantly before she managed regretfully to pull herself away. As she stepped through the doors out into the sunshine her mind was still far away. It would not have surprised her at all to find the city of Helena magically converted to its 1880 condition, streets full of cattlemen, miners and cowpokes.

She smiled at herself as she moved down Roberts Street toward her motel. She was getting far too strong an imagination. It was fine to think about the old days, but she must not expect to find *that* West. Not any more. It had been vanishing when Charlie Russell strove to preserve it. And it was gone now, for sure.

Melinda flexed her aching shoulders and slowly swiveled her neck. Her body was tired and hungry, and her mind seemed numbed with so much input. What she needed now was a little relaxation, something different to rest her mind.

As she stood waiting for the light to change, the roar of a motor came out of the street behind her. Melinda paid it little attention; her thoughts were on her empty stomach. First she would eat—

The roar of the motor grew louder and a cycle came round the corner and skidded to a stop beside her. Melinda drew back in surprise, startled by its sudden appearance. The man on the bike took off his helmet. "Fancy meeting you here," Cal said in a good imitation of Cary Grant.

For a moment Melinda could not move. He couldn't be here, materialized out of thin air right here on the street in Helena. She'd left him in Broadus, left him with no notion of ever seeing that tanned strong face again. And there he sat, grinning mischievously and every bit as attractive as she had remembered him.

He waved a dark hand in front of her eyes. "Hey,

Melinda. It's me. Cal. Remember?" The black eyes
regarded her quizzically.

"Of course I remember," she replied. "But—but—"

"What am I doing in Helena?" he asked.

She nodded. She was swept with alternate waves of
confusion and joy. She was very glad to see him and yet
she did not want to be.

"Same thing I'm always doing. Enjoying myself. I saw
this beautiful girl afoot and I thought I'd take a look." His
eyes twinkled. "Thought there was something familiar
about the way she walked. And there you were. Hop on.
I'll give you a ride."

Melinda stared at him. "On that?"

He grinned. "Of course on this. I'm really a very good
driver. Not a thing to worry about. Just tell me where to
go and I'll deliver you safe and sound."

"I—" She was torn. Part of her wanted very much to
go off with this mad cowboy, but the other part kept
reminding her of her resolution. She had no time to mess
around with men; she had a job to do. But, she told
herself, she had spent the entire day working; surely she
had a right to some relaxation.

His grin faded. "What's the matter? You got something
against cowboys?"

She shook her head. She could hardly tell him she had
something against *men*.

"Then get aboard. Time's a-wasting. First I'll take you
back to your room to freshen up. Then we'll put on the
feedbag. Nothing fancy. Us working cowboys don't eat
real high on the hog. Or in this case, the steer. But it'll be
good. I guarantee you that."

She kept telling herself to refuse, to walk away from
him. But somehow she didn't seem able to do it. "My
motel's about a mile away. Straight down the street."
She slung her bag over her shoulder and gingerly
approached the cycle.

"There's nothing to it," he said. "Just swing your leg over there. Keep your feet out of the workings. And we're home free."

As she settled into the seat behind him, she felt the male force of him encompassing her. It gave her a strange heady feeling to be so close to him, to be forced to touch him.

Melinda, who had never before ridden a bike, found herself clutching him round the waist, her cheek pressed hard against his shoulder. The day was warm and he was wearing only a light tee shirt, yet somehow she seemed to scent the faint aroma of leather. She felt the heat of his body, and the muscles under her cheek rippled as he set the machine in motion.

She supposed he was not going particularly fast, but to Melinda the speed seemed tremendous and the ground terribly near. She clung to him in a kind of half panic, her breasts pressed tight against his broad back, her face buried between his shoulder blades.

Moments later she felt the machine slow down. "Which one?" he yelled back and precariously she freed an arm to point. Then they were coming to a stop. For a long second Melinda felt paralyzed, her arms still tight around him.

"You can let go now," he said with a chuckle, and she unlocked her hands and, bracing herself on his shoulder, shakily dismounted.

"There now. That wasn't so bad." He looked her over with a smile that turned suddenly solicitous. "Say, that must have been your first ride."

She nodded, still breathless.

"Doesn't look like you enjoyed it much."

She managed a shaky smile. "It's sort of a shock to go that fast."

He nodded. "You'll get used to it." He grinned again, his teeth flashing white against his dark skin. "I suppose you want me to wait out here while you freshen up."

"Of course." She knew he was teasing her, but she couldn't help blushing a bit.

"Spoilsport."

His banter somehow reminded her of those endless moments on Deadwood's street while his eyes had surveyed her so coolly and completely. Her blood began to pound in her veins.

"Well, I'll be here. Probably in the shade under that tree."

Melinda nodded and hurried off toward her room. She knew she was behaving crazily. Having dinner with this itinerant cowboy, indeed. But it was precisely because of that that he was safe, she told herself. Their meeting was a pure coincidence. She might as well enjoy it. There would be no strings attached. Tomorrow she would get back to work and Cal would be gone.

She pushed that thought away as she hurried to shower and change. Her tiredness seemed to be gone, swept away in excitement at the arrival of the man she had thought never to see again. She dug hurriedly through her suitcase. She had packed several gauze skirts and blouses, mostly because their being wrinkled was part of their fashionable appeal. Now she pulled on a dress of pale blue and slipped her feet into white sandals. She looked at herself critically in the mirror, then ran a comb through her hair, deciding to let it hang free. Grabbing up her purse, she made her way back through the lobby, trying to keep down the impulse to run.

The bike was still parked where he'd left it and under the tree, looking up at the sky, lay Cal. He had exchanged his white tee shirt for a pale yellow sport shirt and his unruly hair seemed to have been settled somewhat with a combing.

She stood looking down at him. For several seconds he

didn't move, gazing up at her in a curious way. "The view is lovely from down here," he said, reaching up to take her hand in his warm brown fingers.

And to her amazement Melinda found herself lying on her back in the grass under the tree. She felt a sense of excitement running through her, a sense of newness and joy, as she gazed up at the slightly stirring branches of the tree and their fresh green leaves.

He didn't turn his head, but his fingers remained wrapped around hers. She did not resist the hard fingers, but let her own lie curled within them. "See what I mean?" he said softly.

"Yes." The word was a mere whisper and Melinda wondered what it was she was supposed to see. The leaves were beautiful, floating so gently in the wind, but she was even more conscious of her feelings, a sort of wonder, of awe, at the beauty of the leaves and beyond and through them the brilliant blue of the sky.

They lay there for several minutes, neither of them speaking, and Melinda felt the tensions of the day draining out of her. It was almost as though something in his hand had pulled them out and they melted away into the earth beneath them.

Then he stood and pulled her to her feet. "We've fed the soul, now to feed the body." He grinned at her. "Do you feel Chinese or Mexican?" he asked.

Melinda hesitated. "I know this is going to sound silly," she said. "But what I'm really hungry for is a big plate of spaghetti and meatballs."

"No problem," he said. "I know just the place. And fresh Italian bread with gobs of butter. A big salad. And a bottle of wine."

Melinda groaned. "I'm starving to death and the man only *talks* about food."

He pulled her toward the bike. "We're on our way. And Melinda—"

"Yes?"

His grin broadened. "Try not to hold on so hard this time. You almost strangled me on the way here."

She felt the blood rush to her cheeks at the thought of being so close to him again. "I couldn't help it," she defended herself. "I was scared. I'm not a very daring person."

"We'll change that," he said confidently, swinging one blue-jeaned thigh over the seat. "Hop on."

Melinda did as she was told, using his shoulder again as a brace. She was thankful for the fullness of her skirt which made climbing on easier. She felt the hard muscles under her fingers as she settled into the seat behind him. It was very difficult not to be affected by so much maleness, she thought, as she wrapped her arms around his waist, her cheek against his hard shoulder. After all, she was only flesh and blood.

By the time they arrived at the restaurant, she was feeling slightly more at ease on the bike. As she was about to dismount, Cal swung his leg easily over the front of the bike and turned to lift her right out of the seat. When he set her down on the sidewalk, she felt as though the hands that had spanned her waist had left a burning mark there. Her blood seemed to be racing madly to all parts of her body and her knees wanted to tremble violently.

"You'll like this place," he said, taking her arm. "I know the proprietors. They're great people."

The restaurant was a quiet little place with an old world atmosphere. A small round woman bustled up to them as the bell over the entrance announced their arrival. "Oh, Mr. Cal! You come see us! We are glad. Right this way. I give you good table."

Cal's hand rested lightly on the back of Melinda's waist as they made their way to a table in a dimly lit corner of the small room.

"You be comfortable here. Papa, he come soon."

"Okay, Mama."

The little woman bustled away and Melinda turned to Cal. "Papa? Mama?"

He smiled and touched his blond hair. "You didn't know I'm Italian? Actually, we're not related. But I've known them all my life, almost. They're like relatives."

"I see." Melinda did not see, not really. But she discovered that she liked the idea of Cal being welcomed here. It made him more real, more human, somehow.

Then a man came hurrying out of the kitchen, the match of the woman. "Mr. Cal! You wait too long come see us. Whatsamatter?"

"I been away, Papa. Doing some riding. You know how it is."

Papa grinned. "I know. I young myself once. And this young lady. I never see her before."

Melinda felt herself blushing but Cal did not seem at all disturbed by Papa's curiosity. "Her name's Melinda and she's a new friend of mine."

"Nice friend," said Papa, his eyes gleaming appreciatively, and Melinda wanted to giggle.

"We'll have the works," said Cal. "Spaghetti with lots of meatballs. Your best wine."

Papa looked disapproving. "Always you get the best wine. You know that." His round face crinkled into a wide grin. "I go now. Make your spaghetti with my own hands." He bowed slightly toward Melinda. "You enjoy."

"They're very nice people," Melinda said, suddenly aware that the restaurant was rather romantic with its white draped tablecloths and glowing candles.

Cal reached across the little table and took her hand in his. "I think so." He stroked the back of her hand, the lightest of touches, and she felt her whole body go warm. "So how is your trip coming?"

"Fine. I spent the whole day at the Historical Society.

67

What a marvelous place." Her face glowed in the candlelight. "It's just—I can't find the words. I think I'd live there if I could."

His fingers moved again on her hand, turning it over. "They've got some great Russell stuff."

Melinda looked at him with surprise. "You know Russell's work?"

Cal nodded his head. "I'm not exactly illiterate," he said, a smile taking the sting from his words. "And remember, Melinda, this is Montana. This is Charlie Russell country. The man's almost one of our state heroes."

Melinda nodded. "Of course. I wasn't thinking."

Their salads came then, and afterwards the rest of the meal, and they were engrossed in eating. The spaghetti was the best Melinda had ever had and she told Papa so. He beamed and brought more wine.

Melinda put her hand over her glass as Cal reached to fill it. "No more for me. I've got work to do tomorrow."

"Yes, of course."

The wine had mellowed her and she went on to tell him about her book. "So you see I've got a lot of work to do—thinking and deciding work," she concluded.

"That's the hardest kind," said Cal. "I'd rather break a wild horse any day."

"Have you done that? Really?" Melinda didn't know that her eyes glowed like twin emeralds in the candlelight.

"Of course I have. I grew up on a working ranch." His eyes took on a distant look. "Those were the best years of my life, the very best. I don't think anything will ever equal them."

Melinda sighed. "I know just what you mean. When I used to visit Gramps— Oh, it was like another world." She sighed again. The wine was making her melancholy. "But that's all gone now. That whole world. Nothing left except what's been captured on canvas."

He nodded in agreement. "But you can't fight change, Melinda. That's the way the world is. Nothing's constant but change itself."

"I know that." She smiled grimly. "But I don't have to like it."

He finished his wine. "Ready to go?"

Melinda nodded. She did not really want to leave this warm and wonderful place. She did not really want to leave Cal. But he was right. The world went on. And people had to go with it.

"See you later, Papa, Mama," he called to the old couple and escorted Melinda to the door. Seeing her look of surprise, he smiled. "We have an arrangement. I pay my tab once a month."

Melinda said nothing. So sometimes he didn't have enough money even to eat. And his old friends stood by him. Well, cowboys had always been like that, she reminded herself. An improvident lot, squandering the wages of a whole season's work in a few short nights. But they were loyal buddies, too, taking care of each other when the need arose.

Silently she climbed back on the bike behind Cal. She was getting the knack of it now, she thought. Now that the evening was almost over. The thought hit her like a physical blow. She did not want it to be over, did not want Cal to step out of her life again. All evening the remembrance of that fleeting kiss of farewell had danced in the back of her mind.

He headed the bike in a direction away from where her motel lay. "Where are you going?" she yelled at him. But he pretended not to hear her. The bike sped through the streets and out beyond the town, up the side of Mt. Helena. Melinda, frightened more by the increased speed of the bike than by Cal's refusal to answer her, clung to him as the bike moved ever upward.

Finally he drew off the road and halted. He stuck his

helmet on the handlebars and climbed off, turning to reach out for her.

Melinda glared at him. "What are we doing up here?" she said stiffly.

"I wanted you to see the lights of the city. Look!" He gestured through the darkness to where the lights of the city twinkled brightly below.

Melinda gasped. "Oh! It's lovely."

Cal smiled. "I've always thought so. I come up here often."

His hands around her waist lifted her from the cycle. For a long moment he held her so, her feet slightly off the ground. Then he gently set her down. "Come over here. You can see for miles and miles." And taking her hand in his he led her toward the railing.

She saw now, as her eyes grew more accustomed to the darkness, that this was a regular place for cars to stop. Evidently many people enjoyed the view of the city below.

Except for the noise of insects, the night was still around them as they looked down toward Last Chance Gulch and the town. The night air was heavy with the scent of pine. For long moments neither of them spoke. Melinda felt Cal's hand drop hers, his arm steal around her waist. She did not draw away. It seemed right, somehow, to stand like this, looking down at the city.

"Look up at the sky," he said finally. "At the stars."

The sky was dark, but every star in the heavens seemed to sparkle brightly. Melinda sighed softly. "This is the most beautiful country. I wish I could live here."

He chuckled. "What about the Historical Society?"

Without thinking, Melinda leaned against him. "I don't know. Maybe I'll take turns. A day in the Society. A day up on the mountain."

Cal's arm tightened around her. "You've seen the prairie. What do you think of it?"

"It's beautiful," she said. "In a sort of awesome way. It must have been very hard for the first women coming out here. So lonely."

His fingers moved softly at her waist. "It was bad for men, too, that fear of the land, the terrible loneliness. In the old days they called it 'seeing the elephant.' Once you saw the elephant, you were in real trouble."

"I can understand that," Melinda said softly. "There's a grandeur to the prairie. But there's a terrible starkness there, a terrible sense of the power of nature."

They were silent for several minutes, each lost in their own thoughts. Then he put both his hands on her waist and turned her toward him.

Her heart rose up in her throat like a frightened child's and she could only stare up at him. In the moonlight his hair was an almost white halo, but the dark face beneath it, from which those hard black eyes gleamed, made him almost sinister, a force like that of the land itself. Impossible to understand, never to be tamed.

His hands were firm on her waist, strong, and their heat seemed to sear her flesh through the thin material. She could not move; she was being held captive there by the force of his eyes. There was in them all the invitation that they had held that day in Deadwood, but there was more. There was a seriousness, a look almost of intentness, in the gaze that held hers.

And then slowly, almost as though this had been a slow motion scene, he bent his head to hers. She felt her arms slide round his neck of their own volition as he pulled her close against his chest. Her breasts were crushed against his hardness; she thought she could feel the pounding of his heart against them.

Then his lips were on hers. This was no fleeting kiss of farewell, this long intense exploration of her mouth. Melinda felt her body stirring. She wanted this man. She had wanted him almost from that first moment she had

71

seen him, gazing at her with that devilish invitation so open in his eyes. But now she wanted him with an intensity that was terrifying to her. Tom had reached her sensuality; he was, after all, an experienced seducer. But never had she felt the kind of passion she was feeling now, this wild dancing in her blood, this sense of inherent rightness of it all.

His lips lingered on hers, caressing, possessing, teasing. Suddenly fear was strong in her. She couldn't allow another man to possess her. She had promised herself never to go through such a thing again with the certainty of a real emotional commitment. She pushed frantically against his chest, but he ignored her. His mouth was hot and devouring, his arms held her in an inescapable embrace. She twisted her head to avoid his kisses; they landed on her exposed throat, her ears, her cheeks. A sob caught in her throat. She did not want to resist him. Yet she must.

Oblivious to her struggles, he lifted her easily in his arms and strode off into the darkness of a little grove of pines. She did not think of crying out; she had no strength for that. The sobs in her throat were choking her as she fought the desire to press closer against him.

Then they had reached the darkness. In one swift movement he laid her on the pine-needle covered ground and was there beside her, his mouth against hers, his body pressing close.

She tried to roll away from him, but his arm was heavy over her breasts, pinning her against the warm fragrant earth. His mouth moved persuasively against hers, teasing, caressing, stirring the primitive part of her. Through the thin gauze of her blouse she felt the heat of his caressing fingers on her side. She put both hands against his chest and pushed with all her remaining strength, but it was not enough. It made no impression on him at all.

His mouth covered hers, devoured it. Her tongue,

accidentally meeting his, sent off an explosive message to the rest of her body.

His lips became softly persuasive, his hand pulled the shoulder of her blouse down and crept inside to the smooth skin of her breast. The touch was gentle, expert, as he stroked the velvet surface. From her captured mouth a little moan escaped. His kisses grew more urgent and his hands, to which she could offer no more resistance, wandered freely over her.

A sort of madness rose up in her then, a madness that short-circuited the thinking process. It was almost as though she were another person, not the rational Melinda Adams at all, but some savage Indian girl, surprised on the prairie by the man she loved. She could only surrender.

They were both breathing heavily, their bodies straining toward each other, when he drew back. "Not here," he said huskily.

He was on his feet, pulling her up, before she quite knew what was happening. Absently she pulled at her clothes. When he got on the cycle, she automatically mounted behind him.

It was not until they were almost back to the motel that she came to the realization of what she had almost done. Her face burned in the darkness. After all she'd been through with Tom, after she'd promised herself never to be caught again. To let this man almost seduce her. Her teeth caught at her bottom lip. When they got back to her motel she would have to send him away.

She had not counted on anything like that. The magic of the night, the beauty of the scene. The excitement of being with him. She had to recognize that. The night might have been beautiful with another man, but she would not have been carried away.

The cycle took the winding curves at high speed and she clung to him tighter, pressed herself into his back, feeling the heat of his body. Under her cheek the hard muscles tensed as he guided the bike.

She must not let him follow her into the room, she told herself firmly. She simply was not going to get involved with another man. But how could she convince him? She hadn't been putting up much resistance out there. And if he kissed her again— She just wouldn't let him, she decided, as the wind blew her hair out in a long tail behind her. He would have to accept that.

He pulled the bike into a space in the parking lot. Melinda scrambled off as he took off his helmet and hung it on the handlebars. "Thanks for the dinner and the ride," she said, clutching her bag in one trembling hand. "Good night."

She wheeled quickly to move away, but one of his big hands snaked out and grabbed her wrist, swinging her around toward him. The parking lot was well lit and his eyes gleamed harshly, their black depths turned hard. "Good night?"

Her wrist ached from the pressure of his fingers and she pulled at them futilely. "That's what I said, 'Good night.'" She tried to make her voice cold and determined, but it broke in the middle of the sentence.

Still he did not release her. Retaining his grip on her wrist, he got easily to his feet. "What kind of joke is this?"

"No joke." She forced the words out. He was too close like this; she was too much aware of his body, of her need to press herself close to him.

"Listen," he said and his free hand in the small of her back pulled her closer yet. "I don't know how they do things in Chicago, but here in Montana you don't lead a guy on."

He pulled her against his chest and her senses were going mad from the feel of him. "I didn't!" she protested. "You—you—"

74

"You accepted my invitation to dinner," he began. "And you wanted—"

"I wasn't aware of the kind of payment you'd expect!" she snapped. She was working up her anger now. It was her only defense against him. He was the one who had started things. "I didn't ask you to take me up the mountain for a scenic ride!" she pointed out sharply.

"But you enjoyed it!"

"The view was lovely," Melinda said with artificial sweetness.

He shook her abruptly, the line of his mouth hardening. "I'm not talking about the view," he grated. "And you know it."

He was very close to the truth, of course, but she felt she had to make some retort.

"You—you didn't give me much choice." She tried to make the words sound bitter.

His mouth grew grimmer and a muscle in his jaw twitched. "Don't give me any of that," he said harshly. "You were willing enough."

"You have a convenient sort of memory," she cried. "You don't seem to recall that I tried to push you away!"

"And moments later you were kissing me madly!"

She was stung by the injustice of it all. "I—I just don't know you."

He shrugged. "What the hell does that have to do with it?"

She shook her head. "I couldn't expect you to understand."

"I understand all right." His drawl deepened. "I've gone and got myself messed up with a tease. Well, lady, that's it. Just let me warn you." He glared down at her. "Don't push your luck too far. Up there on the mountain—" His hands gripped her waist tightly. "I could have had you. And you damn well know it! Next time maybe the guy won't think of your comfort like I did. Better be prepared for that."

Melinda tried to stop the shivering that had overcome her. "I—I'm not what you said," she stammered. "I—I'm sorry."

"Sorry!" He stared down at her sarcastically. "That does it. I'm getting out of here before I go crazy too. Pleasant dreams!"

He dropped his arms from around her and vaulted back onto the bike, slamming the helmet on his head. Seconds later he was roaring away.

For a moment longer Melinda stood there, shivering in the warm night air. What a mess she had made of the whole thing—a real mess. With a sob she turned and made her way to her room—alone.

5

~eeeeeeeeee~

By morning Melinda had calmed down somewhat. Last night had been quite an experience, she told herself as she threw back the covers and went to wash. In spite of her affair with Tom Ryder, or perhaps because of it, she was basically unused to dealing with men. Before Tom she had been so busy with her schooling and her career that she had never been seriously entangled with anyone. The men she had known had all been as engrossed as she with the complexities of earning a degree and finding a position. In graduate school macho men with their ever-questing eyes soon fell by the wayside. There just wasn't time for that kind of thing.

As she pulled on a soft cotton shirt and a pair of cool slacks, Melinda sighed. Actually, she had never seen a man who could affect her as Cal did. With Tom she had felt a kind of comfort. Oh, there had been sexual feelings; he was smart enough to raise them. But there had never been this wild racing of the blood, this trembling that she felt whenever Cal was near.

She attacked her rich chestnut hair with the brush,

almost as though she could vent her feelings about Cal on it. That was the trouble, though, her feelings for Cal were so mixed. She enjoyed his company and yet she feared it. She wanted to be with him and yet she didn't.

She pulled her hair back in a rubber band and made a face at herself in the mirror. No sense in worrying the situation around anymore. Cal had been really angry last night. So angry she never expected to see him again. That was probably best, she told herself, though a small voice inside her insisted that she didn't want it that way. If she didn't see him again, she wouldn't be tempted to throw herself into his arms. A very real temptation, she thought grimly as she grabbed up her bag and keys. It was a good thing she had planned to go to the Marsden Collection again today. Sitting around mooning over some dumb cowboy wasn't going to solve anything.

As she inched the red Camaro out into traffic after a quick breakfast, Melinda again considered Jim Pederson. The Marsden Collection was a very necessary part of the book, there was no denying that. Especially as she wanted to use that hitherto unknown painting of branding. Therefore she couldn't afford to alienate Pederson. But neither did she want him to get any romantic ideas. She would have to walk carefully; watch her step. "Like a feller in rattler country," as Gramps would have said.

Melinda swallowed over a sudden lump in her throat. How she missed Gramps. After all these years he still held a big place in her heart. She could see him now with his dirty battered Stetson pushed back on his head, his long white moustache yellowed by tobacco but still light against the contrasting darkness of his face. The calloused hands that had braided a little girl's unruly hair as easily as a rawhide. And with Gramps, always, she remembered Lefty, the bowlegged, nondescript little man with the marvelous fund of stories. Between the two of them they'd kept her entertained for long hours, sitting on the veranda between them while the sun slowly set and the old West came alive before her childish eyes.

As she parked the car across from the great Victorian mansion, Melinda felt her excitement rising. No matter what else was going on in her life, to have access to so much of Russell's painting was exciting.

Carruthers opened the door moments after she had pushed the bell. He looked his immaculate butlerish self, but today he allowed the merest touch of a smile to curve his stern lips. "Good day, Miss Adams. Mr. Pederson told me to expect you. You're to go right up."

"Thank you, Carruthers." Melinda had to curb the impulse to giggle. There was something so extremely proper in Carruthers that it inevitably brought out the imp in her. She made her way slowly toward the elevator, admiring the great hall as she went. One thing about those old Montana pioneers, no matter how they made their money—mining, ranching, railroading, gambling, merchandizing—they most certainly knew how to spend it.

As the little elevator creaked slowly to the third floor, Melinda let herself imagine it filled with people of the past. The past had a strong hold on her. She knew that. Perhaps it was because of Gramps and his stories. Perhaps it was because the past was so present here, in a state where preservation societies and historic markers were everyday affairs. She really did not know—or care. She only knew that the past *was* important to her—and to a lot of other people, too, otherwise there wouldn't *be* those societies and markers.

She smiled to herself. She loved this old house. All its "gingerbread," its ostentation, might have been too much in its own day for cultured visitors from overseas. She had read more than one condescending English account of nouveau riche American "palaces." But there was nothing wrong in being proud of what one had accomplished, of coming up from nothing as so many of these people had.

When the elevator ground to a slow halt, she discovered Jim Pederson standing on the other side of the grill, wearing a big beaming smile. Melinda smiled herself as the door opened and she stepped out, a friendly smile, that was all. "Good morning, Mr. Pederson. Isn't it a lovely day?"

"I thought it was Jim and Melinda," he said, his forehead wrinkling into a frown.

Melinda nodded. "Of course, I'd forgotten."

"And did you have a pleasant time at the Historical Society yesterday?" he asked.

"Oh yes. It was marvelous." She smiled ruefully. "I skipped lunch altogether I was so engrossed. And my feet felt like they were going to fall off."

"But here you are, ready to repeat the same procedure again." His grin conveyed just the right amount of friendliness.

Relaxing, Melinda returned it. "That's about it," she said. "I believe I've gone crazy about Russell's work. I could just stand and stare at it for hours. The marvelous detail. And the color." She laughed. "But here I am telling you. And who should know better?" She sighed. "You know, I rather envy you this job. I suppose it is lonely sometimes." She noted his vehement nod. "But to be able to be around all this every day." She shook her head. "I just can't imagine anything so wonderful."

Jim Pederson's smile disappeared. "It is a marvelous opportunity," he said. "And I'm grateful for it. But I've been here quite a while. And the truth is we human beings are a strange lot. We just don't appreciate things when we have easy access to them."

Melinda was considering this when the phone rang and Pederson moved to answer it. She heard him mumbling replies and moments later he was back at her side, smiling ruefully. "I'm afraid I'll have to leave you today. Something's come up that I've got to check on. But you know your way around. Make yourself at home."

Melinda nodded. The truth was that she did not at all mind Pederson's leaving. In fact, she would be pleased to be alone with the collection. She got out her tablet and pen and began to work.

She had no idea how long she'd been engrossed, moving from painting to painting, standing lost in thought before each marvelous canvas, when the sound of an opening door caused her to turn. The smile of greeting which she had put on for Pederson's return faded. The man that stood before her, a man in an impeccably tailored summer suit, his shirt startlingly white against his bronzed skin, was not Jim Pederson.

"You!" The word burst from Melinda's throat. "What are you doing here?"

"Good morning, Miss Adams," the cowboy Cal replied in coldly polite tones. "Are you enjoying the Marsden Collection?"

"Of course I am." Melinda was confused. What was this man doing here? And dressed the way he was? "Mr. Pederson isn't here right now," she said. "I'm sorry, but you'll have to come back."

His smile was a grim line in his dark face. "I know that."

"You do? But how?" Now she was even more confused.

"I know because I sent him out. To run an errand for me."

"For you?"

He nodded, his eyes like pieces of black jet. "Yes, for me. Perhaps I should introduce myself more formally. Colin Marsden." He extended a hard brown hand.

Melinda gasped and took a step backwards. "Colin Marsden! You can't be. You're—you're a cowboy. A biker."

He withdrew his hand and smiled dryly, but no hint of amusement appeared in those dark eyes. "So what? I'm still Colin Marsden."

Melinda felt the blood stain her cheeks. This man, this man she had imagined to be an itinerant cowboy, not always able to pay his bills, this man was the renowned Colin Marsden. Then suddenly her dismay was replaced with anger. He had known. Last night she had talked about the book, about coming here. And he had not revealed himself. He had let her go on, not knowing who he was. She drew herself up rigidly. "You deceived me," she said coldly. "Why didn't you tell me who you were?"

Again he smiled, the almost sinister smile of a man about to impart bad news. "And *then* you would have treated me differently, I suppose."

"No!" Melinda's response was immediate.

His twisting mouth showed his disbelief. "I learned long ago not to advertise myself," he said. "Why do you think I go around as Cal? It's safer that way. At least the women want me for my body, not my money." His laugh was harsh and Melinda winced.

"*I* wasn't after either," she cried without thinking.

His expression did not change. "So I discovered. My evening had a peculiar conclusion." He brushed an invisible speck of lint off his coat sleeve and her eyes were drawn to the handsome line of his profile. "At any rate, you've no cause to complain. You're still here, viewing the Marsden Collection, after you refused me."

She nodded. She was too upset and uncomfortable to think clearly. He was being kind about that; he could easily have had her turned away. But why hadn't he?

"That—" She stumbled over the words. "That *is* kind of you."

He shrugged his broad shoulders, wrinkling for a moment the perfect line of his expensive jacket. "I'm not so dense that I can't recognize a genuine love for art. I can respect that no matter how you feel about me."

"I—it seems we got off on the wrong foot—again," she said, hoping to evoke a little smile from him.

His face did not change. "That appears to be habitual with us," he replied. "But never mind, Miss Adams. Your access to the collection will not be hampered, no matter how poorly you behave with me."

"Poor—" She stopped, trying to control her returning anger.

He nodded coolly. "But, so that you might see what a genuine art lover I am, I am determined to give you every assistance in your work. At the other end of the hall Carruthers has set up a desk and chair for your use. I hope you'll be comfortable there. If you need anything, just ask him for it."

"But I can't—"

He looked at her coldly. "I thought your interest in Russell was genuine."

"It is!"

"Then don't turn your back on my offer to help you. I am, sometimes to my own regret, a rather important man in art circles. I can help you a great deal."

The silence was heavy. Melinda's heart pounded in her chest. How could she stay here and work in a room where this man might appear at any moment? In spite of her anger over his high-handedness, she still found him very attractive. To be near him every day would be dangerous. Yet how could she walk away from the chance to work with so many paintings? And Marsden *was* an important man, important enough to get all the collections in the state closed to her if he wanted to.

"I—" She had to try three times before she could get the words out. "I thank you. That is generous of you."

His black eyes danced dangerously, as if he knew what the words cost her, but his tone was even. "I, too, admire Russell's work," he said. "And my grandfather was one of those cowboys whose story you want to tell. It's only natural that I should be willing to help you."

She nodded. There was more to this than his words indicated, she knew that with deep certainty. But she could not say exactly what. "Very well. Thank you."

"Come and go as you please," he continued. "I may be working over there." He indicated one of the desks in the corner. "When I'm not enjoying myself out in the wide world, I spend a lot of time searching for paintings for the collection."

Melinda nodded, feeling her cheeks redden again. Her embarrassment was becoming overwhelming. It was clear she had much underestimated the man. Still, she told herself angrily, it was his own fault. How was she to know that the dusty cowboy Cal was Colin Marsden?

With one last look at her he turned and went off to his desk. Quickly Melinda moved toward the corner he had designated as hers. She hoped that it would be screened from his view. But, though it was the length of the big room away from him, it was still within his sight. She set her purse down hurriedly and moved back among the paintings.

She took great care to keep her back toward him and to stay at a distance. But even when she stood before paintings which, because of the arrangement of the room, were completely hidden from him, she thought she could feel those black eyes boring into her back. He never said a word, however, and when sometimes her eyes happened to stray that way, he always seemed busily at work. She would simply have to get used to his presence, she told herself, as she stopped before one of her favorite paintings.

"The Challenge" depicted two great stallions in battle over possession of the wild herd that could be glimpsed in the background. The painting had captured Melinda's heart, but working it into the book presented something of a problem. It really didn't fall easily into any of the chapters she had outlined.

She sighed, made a note, and moved on. She would give it more thought. She paused before "Rider of the Rough String." There was no question where this painting would fit. It showed quite graphically one of the many risks the cowboy ran every day.

There were a great many paintings showing Indians. Melinda had already chosen two, "Our Warriors Return," and "Breaking Camp," which she planned to include in the book. But she knew that her story wouldn't be complete without some that showed the fighting. That *had* happened between cowboys and Indians, though not nearly with the frequency that the movies and TV seemed to indicate.

Gradually everything faded from Melinda's consciousness but the great paintings before her. So it was that she jumped a little and made a startled sound when she turned to find Colin Marsden standing beside her. So startled was she, in fact, that when she moved she caught her heel in the thick carpet that covered the gallery floor and almost fell. Two strong arms reached out to grab and steady her and Melinda's heart began to pound dangerously.

She raised her eyes to his, but she was incapable of saying anything in those moments when all she could think of was the feel of his hands on her arms.

"I didn't mean to frighten you," he said in that tone of politeness that seemed doubly chilling while his hands were still upon her. "All right now?"

She nodded and he let his hands fall away.

"As I came over to tell you, it's noon. Lunch will be up in a few minutes and I thought perhaps you'd like to wash first."

"Lunch? I can't—" Speech seemed to have returned with the falling away of his hands and she made the protest automatically.

"I'm sure that in exchange for the favor of working here you could condescend to lunch with me," he said dryly. "I find the company of most women cloying. Your reaction to me is—shall we say—almost refreshing. And at least honest."

A shiver went down Melinda's spine. If he really knew her reaction to him—how the sight of him made her grow alternately cold and hot. How she had spent a large part of the previous night regretting having sent him away. How even now she longed to move into the arms that her body remembered with so much pleasure. She found suddenly that she could no longer argue. "Of course," she said, matching her even tone to his.

His nod was almost curt. "There's a washroom through there," he said. "Carruthers should be here with lunch by the time you're ready. He is extremely punctual." The slight curving of his lips indicated that he was aware of Carruthers' more amusing qualities.

"I'll try not to delay him," Melinda said, striving for a measure of lightness. They could not continue to speak to each other in these gravely formal tones like a couple of complete strangers.

His eyes seemed to twinkle slightly, but he merely inclined his head.

As she left the washroom moments later Melinda heard the soft whirring of the little elevator and knew that she would not keep Carruthers waiting. Marsden seated her at the small linen-covered table. Her pulse jumped as his hand brushed her shoulder while pushing in her chair.

She almost thought she could feel his warm breath on her neck.

"I lunch rather lightly," he said as he took his seat. "I find that too much lunch leads to a sleepy afternoon."

Melinda nodded, forcing her lips into a small smile. "That seems sensible."

The table was correctness itself, even to the vase of fresh-cut flowers, and Carruthers served with enough aplomb for a ten-course dinner. Because of his presence, Melinda found herself better able to carry on a conversation with her host. "You must consider yourself very fortunate," she said as Carruthers served up the cream of cauliflower soup, "to live in such a beautiful home."

Marsden nodded. "I do." He smiled ruefully. "Though I'm aware that some people think of it as a Victorian monstrosity."

"Oh no!" Melinda was quick to defend the old place. "It has its own sense of dignity. I waited for Mr. Pederson in the drawing room, the one with the interesting painting over the fireplace," she added. "Now that room should be a national treasure. It's just wonderful." She could not know that her face glowed with her pleasure at the memory or that the man across from her found that glow singularly attractive. She sighed. "There'll never be beautiful places like this again. I'm so glad you can keep it just as it was."

This last thought brought to mind the image of Nicole Erin. And with it the devastating thought that the house would never be safe in her hands. Melinda hoped her face had not betrayed her feeling of revulsion at the thought.

"It is a pleasant room," he agreed. "My mother was extremely fond of it. Actually, this was her father's home. He built it when he struck it rich."

"In the gold fields?" inquired Melinda politely.

Marsden shook his head and his smile was slightly cynical. "Afraid it was nothing so romantic. Grandpa Gerhart was a merchant. Made his pile from scratch. Just as my father's father built his ranch out of nothing."

Melinda sighed. "You can't do that anymore. The old West is gone."

She found that Marsden was looking at her curiously. "You're a very romantic person," he said. "Sure, the old West was exciting, but it was dirty—and crude." There was something about the way he said the last two words that reminded her of those moments on the street in Deadwood. "A lady would have been uncomfortable in the old West. Unless she had a strong man to protect her."

With his use of the word "lady" she was sure he meant her to remember their more intimate encounters, both in Deadwood and on Mt. Helena. Melinda wished fervently that she could keep herself from blushing, but she felt her cheeks grow warm and she saw from the look in his eyes that he knew the cause. "I suppose so," she murmured, unable to think of a sharp rejoinder.

Carruthers served them each a garden salad and set a tray of elegant sandwiches and a bowl of fresh fruit on the table. "If that'll be all, sir?" he murmured and Marsden nodded.

Melinda found herself alone with her host. She cast about in her mind for something to talk about, anything to keep the conversation from personal matters. "How do you feel about having all these treasures sort of locked up here?" she asked. "Wouldn't it be nicer to decorate your house with them?"

Marsden looked thoughtful. "It might be. But I knew an old Chinese man once. He gave me a new insight on precious things. The Chinese, he told me, don't keep their treasures sitting out like Americans do. Whatever they have that is precious and beautiful they keep wrapped up, stored away in chests. Whenever they want to view it, they take it out. Then afterward, they wrap it up again."

"But how can they appreciate it like that?" Melinda asked, intrigued in spite of herself by such an idea.

Marsden shrugged and reached for a sandwich. "I don't know. He seemed to think that when you have things sitting around all the time you soon stop seeing them. Every time the Chinese unwraps his treasure, it's as though he bought it anew."

Melinda chewed her deviled crab sandwich thoughtfully. "I never thought about it like that before. It sort of makes sense."

Marsden nodded. "So I've thought. And I've seen the gallery here as something like that." He smiled and this time the light of it barely reached his eyes. "I do on occasion put some favorite in my bedroom for a while. But I rotate those so I don't quit *seeing* them."

"That seems like a good idea." Melinda swallowed a sigh with her bite of sandwich. It was very trying having him behave so politely, especially as the air between them was thick with tension. She knew she was not imagining that, nor the heat in those black eyes when he thought she wasn't watching him. She supposed she must be some kind of puzzle to him. A challenge even. A woman who had not succumbed to his considerable charm. She was very much aware of that charm, however. So much so that her body was constantly reminding her of its attraction to him.

He finished his sandwich and raised his eyes to hers. "Tell me some more about your book," he said, taking a banana from the bowl.

"I—it's going to be about Russell's work. At first I thought about using other artists, especially Remington. But now I've decided to stick to Russell. He's done so much and it's all so good."

The glow came over her face again and Marsden leaned back slightly in his chair, the rigid lines of his mouth relaxing as he munched the banana. "How did you get so hooked on Russell?"

"Grandpa knew him," she said. "He and Lefty used to talk about him now and then." Her eyes took on a faraway look. "They used to tell me the most wonderful stories about the old days. About the hard, dirty, lonely life of the cowboy," she explained, telling him of Gramp's ranch in Havre and her childhood visits.

"And that's what you want to put in your book." His eyes had softened with understanding.

"Yes. I want people to know what it was really like." She paused. "Of course I realize that the myth of the cowboy isn't going to be changed overnight. For one thing, not that many people are going to read an art book. But at least I'll have had my say. And somewhere some people will come to love Charlie Russell's West as much as I do."

He nodded gravely and she could not help feeling warmth for this man who did not discount her ideas or her affection for the old days, this man who was infinitely more of a man than Tom Ryder. Melinda searched her memory for Tom's features and discovered that they were quite vague. He really meant very little to her now and she wondered how he could ever have been the center of her life.

Secure in the knowledge that Marsden understood her and knew what paintings she was referring to, she went on to tell him about the first chapter.

He nodded. "What do you plan to use on the cover?"

She hesitated. There it was, her golden opportunity to ask him if she could use "When Branding Comes Round," but she could not do it. "I—I haven't made up my mind yet," she stammered, averting her eyes from those probing black ones that seemed almost to be able to read her mind.

Though the lines around his mouth tightened a little, he did not pursue the topic. Instead, he glanced down at his watch. "Sorry, but I have to run. Big meeting in an hour." His smile was a little more genuine. "Make yourself at home." He pushed back his chair.

For a moment he stood there, towering over her, and Melinda felt a tinge of fear. He was such a big man, so full of power. She got to her feet and faced him. At least she *felt* less vulnerable that way.

"By the way," he said. "Carruthers will serve lunch every day at noon."

She opened her mouth to protest and he frowned at her. "He will serve it whether you eat it or not. It does seem a shame to have good food go to waste. Some days I may join you. On others I may not. Enjoy yourself."

He swung on his heel and strode off. For a long moment Melinda allowed herself the luxury of an uninterrupted look at him. What a great-looking man he was, she thought, her teeth unconsciously worrying her lower lip. With those broad shoulders and lean hips, the striking contrast of his sun-bleached hair and his bronzed face, that air of arrogance that surrounded him wherever he was. No wonder he didn't advertise his real identity. All that money and such good looks, too. Women must be after him all the time. But she had liked him better as a poor cowboy, even though he'd been arrogant then, too.

With a sigh she turned back to the gallery. It would seem lonely up here without him, she thought, and wondered momentarily if Jim Pederson would return. When she realized that she hoped not, she knew it wasn't loneliness that was bothering her at all, and turned hastily back to her desk to work on Chapter Two.

It was four-thirty when she pushed her chair back with a sigh. Secure in the feeling that Marsden would not return, she had long ago kicked off her shoes. Now she wiggled into them again and spent a moment rereading her notes. Tomorrow she would bring everything here and set up this desk. A little quiver raced down her spine. Probably he wouldn't even be here, she told herself. And even if he was, it meant nothing. It would be foolish of her to forego working here when she had such a chance.

For a moment she let her thoughts linger on Colin Marsden. For some reason she could no longer think of him as Cal. That dusty cowboy seemed another person altogether. Yet she had to admit that no matter what he wore—blue jeans and boots, or expensive suit—he was still terribly attractive. Strength and vitality seemed to emanate from him, along with that sexual magnetism that drew women like flies. Melinda smiled. The simile was not badly chosen. Except where did that leave that spider Nicole Erin?

Melinda shook her head. She could not imagine herself marrying for money or prestige, but surely that was Nicole Erin's aim. She did not seem capable of real love, so what else could she expect to get from such a union? Surely she did not expect to have *his* love? Such a man, if he ever came to love, would do it fiercely, thought Melinda. With the power and energy that he put into all his efforts. There would be no "someday" fiancée. He would want her *now*. And that would be one very lucky woman.

Melinda found her fingers clenched into fists and flexed them. There was certainly no use in getting romantic ideas about Colin Marsden. He was so far out of her class that it wasn't funny. And besides, she reminded herself, though she seemed to be forgetting it more and more often these days, she had no time for men. Her career was to be the center of her life now. And, jamming her notes into her purse, she moved toward the little elevator.

6

~~~~~~~~~~~~~~~~~~~~

The days passed swiftly. One day, two, three, Melinda spent in the old ballroom, surrounded by paintings. The desk in the far corner of the room soon grew cluttered with her notes and the pages of her manuscript. It was all going very well and she would have been quite happy if it hadn't been for the disturbing presence of Colin Marsden. He actually did nothing to annoy her. He worked very quietly on his side of the room while she worked on hers. He did not stare at her. Though she often thought she felt his eyes upon her, when she glanced his way he was always hard at work.

Except during lunch, they spoke only to greet and leave each other. And the lunch hour, which seemed all too brief to Melinda, was always given over to purely intellectual conversation—a discussion of the work of other, older, Western painters like Frederick Remington or of contemporary artists like Fred Oldfield, or some event in Montana's colorful past.

Melinda had to admit that she enjoyed those conversations, enjoyed them immensely. For never before had she had such an opportunity to discuss the art closest to her heart with anyone knowledgeable. It was a rare privilege and her eyes sparkled with the delight of it.

Sometimes she and Marsden got into rather heated discussions over certain artistic issues and once Melinda cried out defiantly, "If you were an artist yourself, you wouldn't say that."

There was such a look of desolation in the dark eyes looking into her own, that Melinda gasped. "Oh dear, that's it! You want to be an artist."

The look vanished and Marsden's face settled into bland lines. "Wanted," he said, stressing the past tense. "But I couldn't make the grade."

"How do you know?" She wasn't fooled by his attitude. No one could have ignored the pain in that momentary look.

His laughter was forced. "I know. Believe me, I know. I had the best teachers. They all agreed I didn't have it."

Melinda shook her head. "That doesn't matter," she said earnestly. "An artist must have the courage of his convictions."

Marsden raised an elegantly clad shoulder. "Perhaps that's it," he replied dryly. "I had no convictions. No theory." He laughed harshly. "No talent. Just a terrible desire to paint."

Melinda's lunch lay forgotten. "I want to see some of your work."

He shook his head, his expression stern. "Leave it alone, Melinda. The experts were right. I'll never be another Charlie Russell. Now I spend my time collecting the works of others."

Something clicked in Melinda's mind. "The picture downstairs in the drawing room. It's yours!"

Colin Marsden looked very uncomfortable. He seemed about to deny it, but then realized he had already given himself away. "Unfortunately you're right. My mother liked that painting and made me promise to keep it hanging there when she was gone. A promise I've since regretted," he added.

"But it's good!" Melinda's eyes glowed. "It's primitive and a little crude, but it shows promise."

He stared at her, his black eyes gone cold. "I suppose the next thing you'll be telling me is that I'm another Charlie Russell."

"Of course not." His coldness annoyed but did not stop her. "You have a different kind of talent. You shouldn't let it lie fallow."

His smile was grim. "If I didn't know that you rather dislike me, I might suspect that this was a new approach —the way to a man's heart is through his painting."

For a long moment Melinda stared at him across the table. If he just knew how much his physical presence attracted her. It was only by keeping her mind on art that she could keep from concentrating wholeheartedly on her body's insistent response to this man. At that very moment butterflies were filling her stomach. But it wouldn't do to let him know that.

She summoned her iciest frown. "I'm really very sorry, Mr. Marsden, to have upset you by liking your painting. It was terribly stupid of me, I'm afraid. And as for someone finding their way to your heart, I pity anyone who tries. Especially as I'm not even sure you *have* one." With that she pushed back her chair and marched firmly away.

Her hands trembled only slightly as she gathered together her papers. It was impossible to work here now. In fact, she wouldn't be surprised if he denied her access to the collection. And all because she'd told him the truth about his painting.

Unshed tears glistened in her eyes as she began cramming papers in her briefcase. There was a sound behind her. Colin Marsden's hands turned her around to face him. His touch sent her senses spinning, but the way he was glaring down at her caused little shivers down her spine.

"What do you think you're doing?" His hands dug into her upper arms.

"I—I'm gathering my things. I can't work here anymore."

The dark eyes bored into hers and she fought the feeling of being captive. "Nonsense," he said briskly. "Your access to the collection doesn't depend on your relationship with me."

She saw the effort he made to smooth away the frown. His voice grew lighter and she knew that was deliberate, too, as was the lessening pressure on her arms.

"I guess I shouldn't complain if you like my painting." He managed a wry smile. "Though it does put your taste in question."

For long seconds Melinda stood there, her eyes held by his. Her body quivered with pent-up desire. One little touch from him, one word, and she was afraid she would fall right into those strong brown hands. There was warmth in the dark eyes now—banked fires of desire. And if she stirred them just the littlest bit, they would burst into flame. And destroy her in the process, said her mind with bitterness.

But she could not keep her body from being moved by the nearness of his. Her knees trembled and butterflies fluttered again in her stomach. Her mouth seemed suddenly dry and she moistened her upper lip with the tip of her tongue. She desperately wanted his kisses; she knew that, but she seemed powerless to move, and warning signals kept sounding in her brain. His eyes seemed to probe her very soul and for a second she felt him lean toward her. Her lips parted in unconscious anticipation.

And then his hands fell away from her arms, fell so

swiftly that she felt a sense of loss, a sense that was further intensified by his quick step backward. "You will continue your work, won't you?" he asked formally. "This is an important book you're working on. I should hate to see you give it up."

Melinda found her voice. "I—I'll stay," she said.

"Good. That's settled." He glanced quickly at his watch. "I'm afraid I've got to run. I'll see you tomorrow."

The last was half statement, half question and Melinda nodded. "I'll be here."

She was still standing there when the door closed behind him. For a long, bemused moment she shut her eyes and let herself go back in memory to that night on Mt. Helena. It wasn't at all difficult. The heat of his body against hers, the feel of his searching kisses, the sweet caresses of his strong brown hands. She gave a long shuddering sigh and opened her eyes. Those kisses and caresses had come from a cowboy named Cal, not from the rich and arrogant Colin Marsden. With a look of grim determination she turned back to her work.

The rest of the day passed very slowly and Melinda found it almost impossible to concentrate. The slightest sound brought her head swiveling around. But Marsden did not return. Finally the hands of her watch reached five and with a measure of relief she picked up her purse and turned toward the door. Maybe she'd watch TV or take in a movie. Anything to get Marsden off her mind. She supposed, she thought as she stepped into the little elevator, that he did have some justification for his behavior. It couldn't be pleasant not knowing if you were wanted for your money or yourself. That could make a man bitter. But *she* was not a fortune-hunting harpie. In fact, she wished he really were that itinerant cowboy she had imagined him to be. It was that man who had crept into her heart. With him she might have had a chance.

But with millionaire Colin Marsden—her grim laughter echoed in the little elevator.

Seeing Carruthers in the lower hall, she gave in to a momentary whim. "Do you suppose I might go in the drawing room for a while? There's something in there I'd like to look at."

"Of course, miss." Carruther's bearing was properly correct, but for some reason Melinda felt that she had his approval.

She entered the drawing room slowly, savoring every detail out of the past, from the lace curtains at the windows to the old-fashioned photographs on the walls. Everything in the room was of a piece. It would be quite easy to believe that she had been transported to the past.

But she turned her attention to the main thing she had come into this room to see—the painting over the fireplace. She studied it for several minutes, white teeth absently worrying her bottom lip. Then she heaved a sigh. She had been right. He did have talent. Some talent. He would never be another Charlie Russell. But he could paint.

Melinda made a face in the empty room. Proving it to him would be next to impossible. With one last lingering look around the room, she turned toward the door, only to have it thrown open with a bang.

"So there you are!" An angry Nicole Erin stood framed in the doorway.

Melinda's eyes took in the expensive dress, the wispy sandals, the mink jacket. Mink in mid-summer, she told herself with a touch of cattiness. However, there was no hint of anything in her voice when she replied, "I was just leaving."

Nicole Erin stepped further into the room. Behind her, in the hall, Melinda caught a glimpse of a hovering Carruthers.

"I want to talk to you," said the other woman.

Melinda raised an eyebrow. "I can't imagine anything we have to discuss."

Nicole's red mouth twisted into a vicious smile. "Well, I can—Colin."

Melinda stifled an urge to laugh. Miss Erin was at least direct. "I have nothing to say about Mr. Marsden. Now, if you'll excuse me."

"Not so fast."

For a fraction of a second Melinda thought the other woman might strike her and she had a vision of the two of them engaged in a knockdown battle in the lovely room. She couldn't let that happen. "Yes, Miss Erin?" She kept her voice calm and quiet.

"I want you out of this house!" The venom in her voice was deadly.

Melinda stifled a sharp retort. "As I said before, I was just leaving."

"I don't mean tonight. I mean for good!" Miss Erin's tone escalated sharply. Evidently she didn't care who heard her. "I've had more than enough of your kind swarming around Colin." The mascara-rimmed eyes glared at her.

Melinda could hardly believe her ears. Too bad Colin couldn't hear this. He would certainly set the enraged Miss Erin straight. "I beg your pardon," she replied sweetly, "but I was under the impression that this house belonged to Mr. Marsden. And he has given me permission to work in the gallery."

Nicole Erin's perfectly made-up face twisted savagely. "It's no use your pretending," she hissed. "Whatever you two are doing up there, you're not working. Colin's never been too busy to lunch with me before."

Melinda was aware of her heart's sharp leap of joy, but she kept her attention on the woman before her. "You are quite mistaken in your assessment of me," she said coldly. "I am writing a book about Western art. And whatever you are to Colin—" Perhaps she shouldn't have used his first name, but she couldn't resist the temptation—"I'm sure he would not appreciate your interference in business matters."

Melinda saw the flicker of hesitation as her words hit home, but Nicole was too enraged to be sobered by them. Her red lacquered nails twitched as though they longed to rake across Melinda's face, but she did not move closer.

"I have warned you, Miss Adams. Stay away from Colin. Otherwise you may find yourself in trouble. My father owns a good bit of this state."

For a moment Melinda was stunned. This was unbelievable. Nicole Erin had made a big mistake. Melinda had never been one to take being threatened. "I'm sure that's very nice for you," she said with heavy emphasis. "But it means nothing at all to me. Nor, do I imagine, would it scare Colin."

For once Miss Erin seemed entirely without words. For a long silent moment she glared at Melinda, then with an inarticulate cry of rage, she spun on her fasionably high heels and stormed out.

Melinda, who had unconsciously been braced for a physical attack, heaved a sigh of relief and sank into a chair. She would just give the irate Miss Erin a little time to roar away in her white Mercedes.

So Colin was too busy to have lunch with her, was he? Melinda mulled that over with a soft smile. But then common sense intervened. It meant nothing really. The fact that Colin had lunched with Melinda every one of the days she'd been there only meant that he'd been working on the collection.

He liked to talk art with her. Nicole didn't appear the type to know anything about it. And perhaps he was still a little disturbed by Melinda's refusal of him.

But that was all there was to it. Certainly she wasn't hatching any plots around the man. It *was* curious that Jim Pederson hadn't been in evidence since that day Colin had sent him on an errand. That could mean—

The hesitant clearing of a throat caused Melinda to look up. An apologetic Carruthers stood just inside the doorway. "I believe Miss Erin is gone now," he said.

Melinda grinned and got to her feet. "Boy, what a temper she's got."

The butler's smile was thin. "Yes, miss. That's no secret to us." The sigh that accompanied this last was heartfelt.

"Couldn't Mr. Marsden put a stop to her tirades?" asked Melinda curiously.

Carruthers shrugged. "He doesn't know, miss. All of us—" he paused, obviously embarrassed. "I mean, besides our own jobs, we've all got relatives around here. And Miss Nicole's father—well, he just does what she says. So we don't dare complain. And she knows it. Most of us will probably leave when she becomes mistress here." His expression showed obvious distress. "I shouldn't like to give up my place. Nor the others. But I, for one, don't think I could work under her." He paused. "What you saw today was mild, miss. She can get a lot worse than that."

Melinda shook her head. It was silly to be upset by Carruthers's words. "I can't understand what anyone can see in her."

"Oh, she doesn't yell at Mr. Marsden," Carruthers added.

Melinda managed a chuckle. "I should imagine not. Not now at least."

The butler looked uncomfortable. "I'm afraid I've been very indiscreet, Miss Adams. It's just—that woman upsets me so I hardly know my own name."

Melinda's smile broadened. "Forget it, Carruthers. My lips are sealed."

"Thank you, miss." The butler seemed to regain his aplomb at this assurance. "Will you be working tomorrow, miss?"

Melinda nodded. "Yes, Carruthers. I'll be here bright and early, provided Miss Erin doesn't have me arrested or something."

The hint of a smile twitched at the corners of Carruthers's now properly formal mouth as he closed the door behind her.

Melinda, driving slowly back to her room, wondered if Colin Marsden could possibly consider making that woman mistress of his lovely old house. It seemed inconceivable that he could be so stupid. But of course he had never seen sweet Nicole in one of her angry moods. What an awakening the man was due for.

Pulling into the motel parking lot, Melinda gave herself a brisk shake. Nicole Erin wasn't Mrs. Colin Marsden yet. And until she was, the old house was safe. And so was Colin himself, though Melinda did not allow her thoughts to turn in that direction.

7

❀❀❀❀❀❀❀❀❀

The next morning Melinda faced the day with a combination of reluctance and pleasure. She knew she was being silly about the whole thing. All this thinking about Colin Marsden couldn't change the facts about the two of them. He was a very wealthy society man and she was an art teacher, not exactly poor, but certainly nowhere in his class. For the first time she regretted that her father's various speculations had not left him the millionaire he had thought they would.

Then she laughed at herself. Money would not have given her access to Colin anyway. If she had had riches, she would never have met him at all. She hurried into her clothes and rushed off to breakfast before her rebellious mind could recall those first meetings with Cal. She had work to do and must not dawdle over it, even if its conclusion meant she would no longer see him.

She would miss their art conversations, she told herself as she parked the Camaro outside the mansion some time later. It was that and that only that left her feeling so lost when she thought about leaving Helena.

Carruthers's greeting was politely formal and the gallery was empty when she reached it. Impelled by some nameless yearning, Melinda wandered over to his desk. It was an old desk, ponderous in its oaken dignity, and her hand clasped unconsciously around the back of his chair, seeking the feel of him. Then she turned swiftly away, refusing an impulse to sit in the chair that had held his body. This sort of schoolgirl foolishness had to stop. He was just another attractive man. With determination she moved toward her desk and picked up her work.

It was several hours later and Melinda had finally settled down to accomplish something when the door opened to admit Marsden. He raised a hand in greeting as she looked up and then went directly to his desk. Melinda turned back to her notes, her eyes going of their own accord to her wristwatch. It looked as though they would share another lunch. The thought warmed her and she realized that she was dreading the long weekend ahead when the Marsden Collection was closed to the public. The Historical Society would be open, but she had really done all she needed to do there and the prospect of two days alone in a strange city was depressing. She did not allow herself to recognize that it was not the thought of the days alone, but of the days without Colin Marsden's company that she was finding so dreary.

Her work seemed to go much faster now that he was there, and she wrote rapidly.

Carruthers arrived with lunch exactly on time. Colin was in the washroom and Melinda gave the butler a slight smile as she approached the table. "It looks like Cook has outdone herself today," she commented, her eyes falling on a casserole of cauliflower, carrots and brocoli.

Carruthers allowed himself a slight smile. "Cook is addicted to trying out new recipes, but Mr. Marsden allows them only on Fridays."

"I see."

A deep chuckle sounded behind her and Melinda felt

her skin grow warm. "I do that for the sake of the staff," Colin said, pulling out her chair for her. She felt his breath on the back of her neck and a little shiver sped down her spine. "That way they only have to act as guinea pigs once a week." He smiled as he seated himself. "Actually, no one complains. Cook does an excellent job."

Melinda nodded. "From the lunches I've had, I'd say you have a real gem."

Carruthers finished his serving and departed and Melinda turned her attention to the food. Colin seemed rather quiet during the meal and she found herself wondering if Nicole Erin had said something to him about their encounter. But he did not seem upset, only preoccupied.

The meal was over and they were enjoying their coffee when Colin looked up suddenly and took a deep breath. "I have a favor to ask of you," he said, his mouth twisting ruefully, "and I'm afraid I don't quite know how to go about it."

Melinda's surprise registered on her face and her heart began to pound, but her voice was calm as she replied. "I suppose the best thing to do is just spit it out."

He smiled briefly. "I suppose so. Well, it's like this. I'm having houseguests out to the ranch for the weekend. Sylvester and Ruth Farmwood and Tom and Lily Durham."

He paused and Melinda waited. "Well, I've told them about your book and they're all eager to push their favorite Russell paintings. They're art buffs, you see. Sy and Ruth run a gallery up in Great Falls and Tom and Lily have one in Whitefish. They know a lot about contemporary Western art, too."

His eyes, which had been filled with warmth, seemed to become blandly impersonal. "I have very much enjoyed our lunch discussions and my friends would love to meet you. They've known each other for so long they know one another's opinions by heart. They'll have a ball with someone new to argue with. That is, if you can see your way clear to coming."

Melinda tried to control the erratic beating of her heart. She supposed that considering the way she felt about him, it was foolish to accept such an invitation, but to turn her back on such an opportunity— She just couldn't do it. Conscious of his eyes on her, she tried to keep her face from revealing too much. "I—That sounds like a lot of fun," she said. "Aside from you, I've never had the chance to discuss Western art with anyone who is knowledgeable about it. Thank you."

He inclined his head politely. "The thanks should come from me." His formal smile was transformed momentarily into a grin. "I'm afraid I'd be in a bad spot if I failed to show up without this expert I've been raving about."

Melinda felt the blood rush to her cheeks. "I'm hardly an expert," she replied.

He cocked one blond eyebrow. "Better not be so modest around your publisher."

The laugh this provoked helped Melinda through her embarrassment. "Why don't you draw me a map," she said. "I'm a visual sort of person and I do better getting places with a map in hand."

It seemed to her that a little of the warmth faded from his smile. "You might as well ride up with me," he said. "It's sort of an out of the way place. I wouldn't want you to get lost."

Melinda swallowed hastily. She hadn't counted on a long ride alone with him. But whatever romantic interest he had had in her seemed to have faded. At that moment she chose to ignore the tension that existed between them. After all, hadn't they been working in the same office for days? And nothing had happened.

His eyes had never left her face. "It's rather a long

ride," he said. "I'd like to leave in an hour or so. If that's not too short notice."

"It is—sort of." Actually, Melinda knew she would be glad for the change of pace.

"I didn't mention it earlier," he said, "because I didn't know for sure till late this morning. The Durhams sometimes have trouble getting help to watch the gallery. We're into the heavy tourist season now and they can't just close down. And one couple won't come without the other."

Melinda nodded, keeping her face carefully calm. It wouldn't do to let him see her excitement. "Where is your ranch?"

"It's up in Charlie Russell country," he said. "I thought you might enjoy seeing that."

"Oh, I would!" Melinda wished she hadn't sounded quite so enthusiastic. "I love the gallery," she added, "and working here. But—" She shrugged.

"All work and no play makes Jill a dull girl," he said, his lips curling slightly. "Here we are in the middle of a beautiful Montana summer and you spend all your days inside."

Melinda smiled. "You captured my feelings exactly." For a long silent moment he surveyed her over his coffee cup, something burning deep in those black eyes, and she had a fleeting sensation that he could sense her other feelings. Then the moment passed. His eyes clouded over and revealed nothing but friendly politeness. "Do you ride?"

"I used to." Melinda's look was rueful. "But it's been a long time."

"It's like riding a bike," he said. "If you knew how once, it'll come back to you." He put his empty cup on the table and glanced at his watch. "Well, I suppose we'd better get moving. If I come by your motel in an hour, can you be ready?"

Melinda nodded. "I think I can make it. Though I should put my notes away."

He shrugged. "Let them lie. No one will be up here over the weekend."

"Won't Jim Pederson be working?" Melinda asked the question casually and was surprised by the sudden hard outward thrust of his jaw. But his words were even enough.

"No. He's out of town, running down a painting."

She got to her feet. "Then I'll just leave everything there. See you in an hour."

Colin's nod was brisk, his chin still belligerent.

Well, Melinda thought as the little elevator moved slowly downward, something had happened to put Colin Marsden off his curator. Of course, if Jim was running down a painting, that explained Colin's working in the gallery—and the fact that he lunched in. She felt the smallest sense of disappointment. It would have been pleasant to think, as Nicole Erin obviously did, that Melinda was the cause of those lunches, but she herself had never really believed it. No, she had made herself very clear to Colin that night outside the motel. And he had ceased regarding her as a potential playmate. And that was a good thing, she reminded herself as she climbed into the Camaro, because otherwise she would not have dared to accept his invitation for the weekend. And she would have been very sorry to miss it.

Once in the motel room, Melinda made a quick assessment of her clothes. Unfortunately she had brought no evening things and she wondered with some annoyance if Colin's guests would dress for dinner. Then she shrugged. If they did, one of her gauze outfits would have to do.

As she packed two pairs of jeans and several shirts, she thought with longing of the boots she'd been admiring after dinner the night before. She had meant to buy herself a pair, but had put it off. Now it was too late.

The suitcase packed, she took a quick shower and slipped into slacks and a shirt. Casting a glance at her watch, she grabbed her hairbrush and went at her hair.

The brush had just joined the other things in her case when a knock sounded on the door. Melinda snapped the suitcase shut and opened the door. Her heart rose up in her throat at the sight of the man who stood there. It was not Colin Marsden, the art connoiseur, but the itinerant cowboy Cal whose tall lean frame filled the doorway. With his worn jeans, scuffed boots and the disreputable Stetson tilted on the back of his head, he looked just as she had first seen him on the street in Deadwood. His eyes slid over her and moved beyond to the suitcase on the bed. "All ready?"

Melinda nodded. "Just the suitcase on the bed." She stepped aside to let him in and, as his sleeve brushed her arm, her body was instantly alert.

He lifted the suitcase and hefted it from one large hand to the other. "You travel light."

She nodded.

"Did you pack your boots?"

"No. I haven't any. I meant to buy a pair but I've been so busy."

"I don't suppose you have a Stetson either." His eyes twinkled at her.

"Not yet," she confessed. "Though I meant to get one."

"Never mind," he said, pulling the door shut behind them. "We'll stop and get what you need."

"But your guests—"

His hand on her elbow guided her down the corridor. "My guests can do without me for a while. They know how to fend for themselves. Besides, I figured you might

110

not have everything you needed so I allowed time to shop."

"You should have told me," Melinda protested. The warmth of his fingers on her elbow was doing strange things to her insides.

He shrugged. "Then you'd have run off by yourself." His grin was tentative, almost as though he expected a rebuff. "And I wanted to go along."

When she did not complain at this, he relaxed visibly. "I know the town. When you're buying basic equipment like boots and a Stetson, you've got to have quality."

"But—but I won't be out here that long."

"Makes no difference," he said. "They'll keep. And the way you love this country you'll be coming back."

Melinda sighed. "I hope so."

He stopped behind a battered station wagon and stowed her case in the back. "Now, it just so happens that right down the street there's a store where we can get what you need."

Half an hour later Cal led her from the store. "But you can't—" she began for the fifth time.

"Simmer down, Melinda."

Her name on his tongue made her nerves quiver with a kind of delight. "But I can't let you—"

"I'll write them off as a business expense," he said with a grin. "Now forget it. It takes time to break boots in. That's why they had to be this good kind. And your Stetson—" His grin widened. "All it needs is a little dust and rain to make it look presentable."

Melinda gave in and smiled. "Maybe we could run over it with the car a few times."

"Now you're getting the idea."

Melinda could hardly believe what was happening. Colin Marsden seemed to have left behind with his business suit the formal behavior he had adopted in the gallery. This was the cowboy Cal she had known before that fateful trip up Mt. Helena. Her heart grew lighter. It was ridiculous to feel so joyful, but she did not seem to be able to help herself.

The afternoon was beautiful and she pushed her doubts to the back of her mind. This weekend was a rare experience and she meant to enjoy it. And as for the boots and hat, though they were far more expensive than she would have bought on her own, she would just send him a check for them—later, after she had moved on. The thought put a momentary damper on her joy, but just then they reached the car.

Letting down the tailgate, Cal unwrapped the boots. "Might as well start wearing them now," he said. Then he untied the box that held the Stetson. "This, too. Maybe if you sit on it for a while it'll get some character."

Melinda, taking the Stetson in fingers that shook, felt the sudden tears trembling behind her eyelids. Carefully she put it on her head.

Suddenly Cal's warm fingers were tilting back her chin. "Let me—" He caught sight of her tears and paused. "What is it, Melinda?"

She shook her head. "I—I was just remembering. The last summer. Before Gramps died. He told me that the next year I'd be big enough to have my own new Stetson." She gulped over the rising sob. "And—and—"

"And next year never came."

Melinda could hold the tears back no longer and they escaped to course down her cheeks. The Stetson was knocked backward off her head and hung suspended by its leather thongs as Cal pulled her into his arms. "Might as well have a good cry," he said comfortably. "My guess is you never did grieve properly for the old man."

Standing there in the circle of Cal's arms, Melinda allowed herself the luxury of great cleansing sobs. When they were over, she felt immeasurably relieved. The sobbing had been reduced to a few sniffles when she finally moved to extricate herself from his embrace. It was not something she wanted to do. For as her grief had abated she had grown more and more aware of the man who was holding her. There was strength in his arms and she found in them a sense of comfort she had not known existed. And a great deal more. Reluctantly she pulled back.

"I'm sorry," she said. "I don't usually carry on like that."

"Think nothing of it," he said as he opened the car door for her. "You can cry on my shoulder—or should I say my chest—whenever you like."

Melinda fished a tissue from her purse and turned toward him as he slid in behind the wheel. "I am sorry," she said. "I don't know what made me behave like that. I feel so silly."

To her surprise his expression grew hard. "You're not being silly. You're being human." The old station wagon sprang to life and for a few minutes he was busy getting it on the road.

When they were out on the street and rolling with the traffic, he glanced at her. "Seriously, Melinda, your reaction is nothing to be ashamed of. Did you go to his funeral?"

She shook her head. "Mother hated Montana. And anyway, they said I was too young."

He shook his head. "Another mistake. Kids should be allowed to learn about death naturally. Did you cry for him?"

"No. I—" She had to swallow before she could go on. "I know it was stupid, but I used to pretend that he was still there—out on the ranch. And someday I'd go visit him again."

He frowned. "If they'd taken you to the funeral, you could have accepted his death. It would have been made real for you. Your crying this afternoon is just an expression of the grief that you never allowed to surface before."

Melinda stared at him. "How do you know so much about the subject?"

He shrugged broad shoulders. "Some of the kids at the Halfway House are unable to show their grief, too. I got interested through working with one of them. Then I kept on studying."

"I see." Melinda let her eyes fall to the boots she was still holding. What an enigma this man was. Not only was he one of the state's richest men and owner of a marvelous art collection, he was apparently a volunteer worker with troubled youths. She smiled suddenly. "I suppose when you go roaring up there on your bike it doesn't do your image any harm."

He gave her a quick smile. "You're quite an intelligent woman, Melinda. In fact, the bike does help. It gives us something in common and makes me seem less stuffy. They can relate easier to somebody like Cal. A business suit would scare them off, to say nothing of knowing who I really am."

"You mean you work with them under an assumed name?"

He shook his head. "No. We just use first names there. And I'm Cal."

"I see. How long have you been working there?"

She did not expect the look of pain that flashed across his face. But she knew she had not been mistaken. "Ten years. Since my kid brother took an LSD trip and didn't come back."

"Oh, Cal!" Her hand went out automatically to touch his arm in sympathy. "I'm so sorry."

His acknowledging nod was brief. Suddenly she realized that her hand was still on his arm and she drew it back, her fingertips tingling from the contact. She felt more tears rising and choked back a sob.

He glanced her way. "It's okay, Melinda. I worked through my grief. And the Stephen Marsden House has helped a lot of kids get back on their feet again. My brother would have liked that."

His eyes regarded her warmly. "Now, you'd better quit holding those boots and get them on your feet. You can't break them in just by holding them in your lap."

Melinda nodded. Not trusting herself to speak, she bent to take off her shoes and pull on the boots. Here was another side to Colin Marsden. Of course it was not unusual for a wealthy man to underwrite some charity. And to bask in the glory of it. But to do volunteer work there, and to do it anonymously—that was something else again. And to think she had believed him a shiftless happy-go-lucky drifter. Red flooded her face at the thought and she kept her face lowered until the blush had faded.

"There," she said, straightening. "Do I look like a Montanan?"

His eyes lingered on her face before they moved down to her boots. "Not yet," he said with a smile. "But you're getting there."

Moving her Stetson out of the way, Melinda leaned back in the seat and relaxed. He had picked up her lead and she knew they would leave the subject of grief behind. She looked out over the rolling countryside. "Where is your ranch?" she asked.

"Northeast of Lewistown," he said. "It's about a four hour drive. We should get there in time for dinner."

Melinda nodded. Dinner with four people she had never met, people who expected her to be an expert. Unconsciously she sighed.

Cal threw her a quick glance. "Relax now and enjoy

the scenery. We'll be going through the Helena and the Lewis and Clark National Forests, some of the prettiest country in the state."

Determinedly Melinda pushed the thought of the evening out of her mind. She would handle that when it arrived. Right now there was all this marvelous country to enjoy. And she meant to do just that.

8

Melinda stirred drowsily. She was having such a pleasant dream—the warmth of Cal's arms around her, the feel of his breath on her forehead. Any minute now his lips would settle on hers and she protested at being wakened from such a lovely dream.

"Melinda, Melinda." The voice was Cal's and it was persistent. Slowly Melinda opened her eyes. There were no strong arms around her, but one was pressed against her side. Or, more accurately, she was pressed against it. She raised her head with a start.

"Easy, Melinda." His voice was reassuring and his hand on her knee was meant to steady her. "You fell asleep. I woke you because I want you to see the ranch from the road."

"Of course." Melinda pushed herself erect and rubbed at her eyes. "I'm sorry I leaned on you like that."

"It wasn't any bother," he said. "In fact, I rather enjoyed it. You look so young and innocent when you're sleeping."

Melinda fought her embarrassment. "Probably my mouth hangs open."

He grinned. "I'm not saying." He slid an arm around her shoulders and she felt the warmth coursing through her. "There's the ranch. The Double M. My grandfather built it from scratch. He was a tough old bird, so they say. But the Marsdens have always been hardcases."

For a long minute she stared at the cluster of buildings sitting far up the dusty road. So this was the place that Cal loved. She could not imagine Nicole Erin willingly spending five minutes in this hot, dusty place.

The parked car was getting warm and Cal reached for the ignition. "So much for your first look at the Double M." He gave her a curious glance. "I hope you don't imagine we're driving into the lap of luxury. This has always been a working ranch. We run a good-sized herd and I breed a few horses now and then. Sort of a hobby, I guess."

Melinda only nodded. Her eyes were fixed on the cluster of buildings that lay at the end of the dusty lane. As they drew nearer, she decided that Cal was right. There were no frills here. No white picket fences. Just a weather-beaten old ranch house. Probably it was the original ranch house—or at least part of it was. The rest had obviously been added as need arose. Yet the whole had a certain unity to it that Melinda relished. "What a beautiful old place," she said.

Cal grinned, clearly pleased by her words. "I like it. I've tried to keep it like it used to be." He smiled ruefully. "I guess we'd all like to keep our childhood."

Melinda smiled. "And you were the one who was telling me how necessary change is."

He nodded. "And if I remember rightly your reply was that you didn't need to *like* it. I guess that's how I feel about the old home place."

"You keep the mansion, too," she reminded him as the station wagon bumped along the rutted road.

"I know, but that's different. The house has historical

value and mother loved it. It was *her* home place, I guess. Even if it meant nothing to me, it should be preserved for future generations. But this place I'm keeping just for me."

Melinda was about to ask how Nicole Erin liked the ranch, but she decided against it. No sense in letting him think she was unduly curious about his affairs. And besides, the less she thought about Nicole Erin the better.

Cal parked the wagon and went around to get her suitcase. Melinda got out and stood staring. The ranch house was big and the nearby cluster of stables, sheds and bunkhouses indicated a good-size operation. Gramps would have loved the place; she knew it instinctively.

Then Cal was beside her, a suitcase in each hand. "Shall we go in?"

"Yes."

Melinda followed him up the steps and across the wide veranda to the screen door. She smiled to see the row of empty rocking chairs lined up waiting. No doubt after dinner guests sat out here, companionably rocking. She was about to move around Cal to get the screen when it flew open and a round little woman came bustling out.

"There you are, Cal. We've been waiting just ages. All on pins and needles to meet your expert!"

She turned to Melinda. "There you are. At last." A pair of merry brown eyes traveled over her. "I see he's been Westernizing you. These men. Sy's been trying these many years to get me into a pair of those horrible things, but he'll never make it. Never. Stetsons now—that's different. I've always thought them rather useful."

"Ruth, you're in Cal's way." A tall thin man, his hair speckled with gray, pulled the round little woman to one side. "Don't mind Ruth, Miss Adams. She's got a non-stop tongue." He smiled affectionately at his wife.

"Please call me Melinda," Melinda said, giving him a

smile. "I'm afraid it's my fault you've been kept waiting. I had to get boots."

Ruth Farmwood's eyes dropped again to Melinda's feet and narrowed shrewdly, but just then her husband spoke. "Tom and Lily are in the kitchen," he told Cal. "Concocting one of their notorious dinners."

Cal groaned. "What is it this time?"

Ruth giggled like a young girl. "We don't know. We've been banned. Maybe you can find out."

Cal smiled. "After I get Melinda settled in I'll give it a try. But I won't make any guarantees." He turned to Melinda. "Let me show you your room."

As she followed him up the wide stairs, Melinda's eyes darted everywhere. The house in Helena gave one the feeling of elegant comfort, an atmosphere of old-fashioned refinement. The ranch house, however, though it was undoubtedly true to its past, did not seem historical. Searching in her mind for adequate words, Melinda could find only one—home. The Double M had an air of being lived in—lived in by happy, active people.

Cal pushed open a door and carried her suitcase across the room to a rough wooden stand. "All the comforts of home," he said.

Melinda, her gaze on the small sparsely furnished room, didn't notice his eyes watching her closely. It was not a woman's room, she thought; no frills, no white curtains. But it had a comfortable feel. She turned a smiling face to him. "Funny you should say that. It *feels* like home."

For a split second something burned deep in his eyes and she felt herself warmed by it. She thought he would move toward her. Something seemed to be pulling them together. Then he shifted abruptly, breaking the spell. "I'll leave you to settle in while I go see what I can learn about dinner. Oh." He stopped and motioned toward a door. "There's a bath through there. Mother liked the amenities of life. It's not fancy, but it's functional."

Melinda, whose heart still pounded in her throat, nodded. "Fine. I'll just freshen up and be down."

"Good."

Then he was gone, closing the door softly behind him. Melinda stood motionless in the center of the room, still held by the tension of those moments. Perhaps she had made a mistake coming here. That look in his eyes— Then she shook her head. She was being foolish. Besides, there were other guests at the ranch. Cal wouldn't try anything with them there. She snapped open her suitcase and took out fresh jeans and a shirt.

Half an hour later, refreshed by a cool shower and a change of clothes, Melinda made her way down the stairs. The living room seemed focused around a huge stone fireplace. She could just see it—the winter winds blowing outside and a great fire turning the room into a haven of warmth. A bearskin rug lay on the wooden floor before the hearth and Melinda caught her breath at the picture her mind had just presented her with—a picture of herself lying in Cal's arms on that rug, a fire casting shadows over their entwined bodies. She didn't have long to consider the fantasy, though, for at that moment the screen banged loudly behind her.

"I thought I heard you come down." Ruth Farmwood's brown eyes twinkled merrily. "Come out on the veranda and enjoy the sunset with us. We have great ones at home, of course, but there's nothing quite like sunset on the prairie."

On the veranda Melinda found Sy in one of the rockers. The one next to him, still rocking gently, showed where Ruth had risen. "Sit there," said Ruth, "and tell me about yourself."

As Melinda settled into the chair, Sy Farmwood chuckled. "You got to watch Ruth, Melinda. She'll have your whole life's history out of you in a matter of minutes."

Melinda smiled. She liked these people. "I'm afraid there's not much to tell. I'm just a college teacher writing a book about the art I love. I'd much rather hear about your gallery and what you have there."

Ruth Farmwood looked disappointed, but her husband smiled. "Cal said you're a real nut on the subject."

Melinda nodded. "I'm afraid he's right. But how can anyone not appreciate a great artist like Charlie Russell?"

A deep chuckle from behind the screen door made all their heads turn. "I told you, Ruth," Cal said as he stepped out onto the veranda. "She'll talk your ear off about Russell. The girl's gone on him." He gave Melinda a smile that made her flesh go goosebumpy.

"That's okay with me," said Sy. "I could talk about Russell for days. I suppose you've seen the uncatalogued one Cal has."

Melinda nodded. " 'When Branding Comes Round.' Yes, it's supurb. In fact—" The words were out almost before she knew it. "I've been thinking what a great cover it would make for my book." Her eyes sought Cal's face, but his expression was unreadable.

Sy nodded. "Sounds like a good idea."

The screen squeaked again and another couple stepped out onto the veranda. "Dinner's almost ready," said a tall thin woman with the blackest hair Melinda had ever seen piled in a great coil on top of her head. A chorus of groans came from the three seated there.

The man beside the woman grinned. "Don't let them scare you, honey," he said, running a hand through thick brown hair. "They're always complaining about our cooking, but I notice they eat it all right."

"It's that or starvation," said the rotund Ruth, pushing at her crisp gray curls.

"Starvation?" said her husband with a chuckle. "Us?" And he looked down at the roundness of his own stomach.

"What great delicacy have you slaved over this time?" Cal asked.

"We've a great new vegetable casserole of cauliflower, carrots and brocoli," Lily began, then paused as Cal and Melinda, their eyes meeting, burst into laughter. "What's so funny?" Lily demanded.

"It's just that Friday is Cook's day to experiment," said Cal. "And today's lunch featured a casserole of—you guessed it—cauliflower, carrots and brocoli. But I suppose we can stand it again."

Melinda, her heart still pounding from that brief intimate second when their eyes had met and held, did not miss the gleam in Ruth Farmwood's eyes at Cal's use of the word "we." Mrs. Farmwood was an inveterate gossip, Melinda guessed, always alert for the smallest scrap of information.

"We also have baked steak with dressing," Lily added. "And for dessert—vinegar pie."

"Vinegar?" Sy and Cal cried in unison.

"Yes, vinegar," replied Tom Durham complacently. "But don't worry about it. It tastes just like custard."

Neither of the men looked convinced, but they said nothing more.

"I think we should wash up and get seated," said Lily with a look around.

Taking the hint, everyone rose and filed into the house. Melinda, following along behind the others, found Cal close behind her. And when she held the door, she was startled to feel his fingers close over hers, imprisoning them against the wood. The rush of warmth that shot through her was so unnerving that she stopped moving. Cal, however, did not stop, at least, not until his body came to rest against hers. She felt the long hard length of him pressed against her and her blood pounded in her veins. God, how she wanted him. Thank goodness, they weren't alone in the ranch house. The feel of him against her was enough to drive all the sense out of her head. And it *would* be senseless to give in to the feelings that were racing through her. She had made up her mind never again to be a man's plaything, any man's.

"Something wrong?" Cal asked softly, his breath tickling her ear.

"No." Sudden panic got her moving and fortunately the others had not overheard their exchange.

The dining room had the same rustic simplicity as the rest of the house and Melinda, allowing Cal to seat her, tried to calm her senses by looking around. Cal's hand, brushing her shoulder as he moved away from her, did not help much. But finally he was seated to her left and a beaming Lily and Tom were putting the food on the table.

"Eat hearty," urged Tom as he took the empty chair to her right.

"Better sample it first," cracked a grinning Sy.

But Melinda wrinkled her nose appreciatively. "It smells just great and I'm starving."

"And here," said Lily, putting a platter on the table, "are the sourdough biscuits. Tom brought the starter from home."

Melinda, helping herself to the steak, noted that in spite of all the teasing, everyone was helping themselves to liberal portions. The noise level dropped measurably as everyone dug in. Melinda found the food excellent and decided that all the razzing must be a kind of in-joke. Even the vinegar pie, despite its threatening title, turned out to be a rather tasty custard.

Lily Durham smiled as Melinda put down her fork and

sighed appreciatively. "That was a great meal. Thank you."

"You're welcome," Lily said. "At least someone here appreciates good cooking." She cast a triumphant look at Cal, who burst into laughter.

"You have to get used to these characters, Melinda," he said, pushing back his chair. "They don't mean half of what they say."

"Unless it's about art," put in Tom. "Then we're strictly serious."

"Speaking of which," said Ruth with a mischievous smile. "Let's go in the living room and talk. We're anxious to pick your brains."

Melinda looked at the dirty dishes on the table. "I'll help clean up first."

"Oh no!" Sy Farmwood's tone was firm. "We have our rules here. Cal should have told you. The cooks also do the dishes and clean up."

"But that doesn't seem fair," Melinda protested.

Ruth chuckled. "Cal should have told you the rules. We used to do it the other way—split it. One couple cooking, the other cleaning up."

Her husband continued. "Until we realized how easy it was to dirty every pan in the place when you know someone else is going to clean them. Now we do our own clean-up."

"And we're more careful," his wife added.

Lily Durham smiled. "We take turns with the cooking," she explained. "So next time they'll do all the work."

"I'd still like to help," Melinda began.

"Against all the rules," both couples chorused. "Very bad precedent."

Cal smiled. "Guess you're outvoted, Melinda. You might as well get used to it. These guys always get their way."

"Why don't you take her for a little walk?" Ruth Farmwood suggested. "Show her the stables." She turned to Melinda. "That way you won't have to repeat yourself. We really do intend to pick your brains."

"They're all Charlie Russell nuts," explained Cal. "So be prepared. Each one intends to push his favorite paintings."

Melinda's smile was genuine. "My goodness. I'll think I've died and gone to heaven. Aside from Cal, I've never known anyone I could talk to about Russell's work."

Sy Farmwood smiled. "You'll get your fill of it tonight. I can guarantee you that."

"Come on," said Tom Durham to his wife. "Let's get busy."

As the two began to stack dirty dishes, Cal rose. "Come on, Melinda."

Her hesitation was only momentary, but she felt Ruth Farmwood's shrewd brown eyes settle on her. "Sure. Let's go."

She took the hand he extended to her; she could hardly refuse it with all of them watching. A shiver went up her spine, but she was not cold. Every inch of her body seemed warmed by the contact of his fingers on hers.

They made their way outside. The sun had sunk lower toward the horizon, but the sky was still a thing of great beauty. Melinda stopped for a moment. "It's—it's breathtaking," she said, indicating the prairie which seemed to stretch out endlessly before them.

"Yes. There's nothing like a sunset on the prairie."

They stood silent for several moments, then he tugged her after him toward the stables. "Come on, there's something out here I want you to see."

Dutifully she followed him inside, the warm smell of horseflesh rising up to meet her.

"Here," he said, rubbing a black velvet nose that

poked out from a box stall at his approach. "Isn't she a sweet little mare?"

Melinda gazed into the mare's liquid brown eyes. "Yes."

"Her name's Countess. I've had her for about a year. Poor thing. She hasn't been ridden much. I don't get out here as often as I like. And when I do, Jericho has to have his turn."

A chestnut head issued from a stall further down and the gelding snorted.

Cal chuckled and moved on. "All right, boy. I'm coming." He pulled Melinda after him. "This is my pet."

The chestnut gazed at her suspiciously, snuffling at the palm she extended to him before he nuzzled it.

Cal grinned. "The old beggar. He wants his treat. Just a minute." He dropped her hand long enough to go into the tack room and return with some sugar cubes.

He put several on Melinda's outstretched palm and she offered them to the horse. Jericho picked them up daintily and chewed happily.

"You've made a friend for life," he said, grabbing her other hand. "Come on, we've got to give Countess some."

Melinda stood happily while the mare took the treat from her palm. She reached up to stroke the dark nose. "She's lovely."

"I'm glad you like her." He seemed about to say something more, but then they heard the crunch of boots on the gravel outside.

"Come on, you two," Sy Farmwood called. "Lily and Tom are about done and we're dying to get at the expert."

"Coming." Cal's hand was warm as it cradled hers and Melinda did not try to escape its hold as they moved back across the rapidly darkening yard. It seemed right somehow to feel his fingers around hers.

A dim light glowed through the open door and Melinda felt a sense of homecoming. She turned to Cal. "Will it be too warm to have a fire?"

He shook his head. "I don't think so. We won't make it too big."

The next hours passed so quickly she could hardly believe it. Lily and Tom Durham, Ruth and Sy Farmwood had obviously been friends for years. They were all older than Cal and they treated him with rough affection as a fledgling, still wet behind the ears. Melinda could hardly believe the way they razzed him, scoffing at his opinions. But even more amazing was the way he grinned through it all, obviously enjoying himself no end.

They teased Melinda, too, though not with quite so much abandon. And each pushed his or her favorite Russell painting as a candidate for the cover.

When Cal looked at his watch and announced, "It's past midnight, we'd better break this party up," she could not believe the time had passed so quickly and pleasantly. She had never before experienced quite the amount of freedom and camaraderie that this evening had brought her.

She looked at the faces around her, the glow of the dying fire reflected in warm friendly eyes, and blurted out, "Thank you for a wonderful evening."

"Thank *you*," said Lily Durham soberly. "We'll remember this night for a long time. We seldom get the chance to have such a good talk." She threw a strange look at Cal as she said this, a look that Melinda noticed and wondered about. But then everyone rose and began to move off toward the bedrooms.

Cal extended his hand to help her out of the deep chair in which she had been curled. She accepted it and he pulled her to her feet. "Wait a minute," he said, scattering the coals of the fire. "We can walk up together."

"All right." Melinda stood quietly, gazing down at his

broad shoulders as he knelt before the fireplace. His light hair caught the last of its glow and gleamed in the dim room. Then the fire was out and the only light came through the big windows, the light of a half moon. It fell across his face as he turned toward her, giving his dark eyes a strange luster. "Ready?"

Melinda nodded. His arm slid companionably around her shoulders, drawing her in against his side. She felt the heat of his body against hers and it was with difficulty that she matched her stride with his. Her first impulse—a wild insane impulse, but very strong—was to swing around into his arms, to feel the long hard length of him against her. To offer her mouth for his kisses.

Melinda curled the hand that was away from him into a fist to keep it from reaching for him. The other, which had slid automatically around his waist as he gathered her to him, rested tentatively on his hip.

They mounted the stairs silently, their feet moving together. Together they moved down the hall. Outside her door, he swung her around to face him and her heart jumped up into her throat.

"I'm glad you enjoyed this evening," he said. "It was a real pleasure for me."

"I did." She barely managed to get the words out.

"Good." He hesitated for a fraction of a second and she thought she felt a tremor in the hands that rested on her shoulders. "Will you ride with me in the morning?" he asked softly. "The others will sleep late. They won't even miss us. I'd really like to show you some Charlie Russell country first hand."

"I'd like that," Melinda replied.

"Let's leave about six. You'll enjoy the early morning."

"Okay." Melinda could not tear her eyes away from his. This was the moment she had been waiting for all evening—dreading, yet wanting it to come.

For a long second there was silence between them and

Melinda thought she could hear the pounding of her heart. She felt her body yearning toward him and she hoped that her eyes did not give away her need.

Then suddenly he withdrew his hands from her shoulders. "See you in the morning. Be sure to wear your boots and your Stetson. And bring a jacket. Good night."

"Good night." The words were a mere echo as she watched him go down the hall and into his room. Only then did she open the door and enter the little bedroom. She didn't know whether she was disappointed or relieved. Probably a little of each, she thought as she slid out of her clothes and into her nightgown. Then she crept between the sheets and fell almost instantly asleep.

9

The clear call of a meadowlark woke Melinda in the morning. With a start she turned toward her travel alarm, but it was only twenty to six. She pushed in the alarm button.

The first rays of the sun were shining in the window and Melinda stretched happily. The morning looked beautiful. Through the window she got a glimpse of the bright blue of the sky, not a cloud marring it.

She threw back the covers and raced across to the open window. The wooden floor was still chilly from the night and she shivered slightly as she looked out across the prairie. It was going to be a beautiful day. An absolutely beautiful day.

She turned from the window and, grabbing up her clothes, hurried into the little bathroom. She washed quickly and slid into her clothes. She brushed her hair vigorously and let it hang down her back. Taking up her Stetson and jacket, her boots in hand, she crept quietly down the stairs. On the porch she paused to pull on her boots. She had worn them the previous evening and they were very comfortable. She shrugged into her light jacket and clapped the Stetson on her head, dropping the leather thongs beneath her chin. Then she moved off toward the stable, anxious for the first ride she had had in many years.

Cal turned as she opened the door, his brown face breaking into a smile as he saw her. "Good morning. Did you sleep well?"

"Like the proverbial log," said Melinda, matching his smile with one of her own.

"Countess is already saddled," he said. "I'll have Jericho ready in a minute."

Melinda moved toward the black mare, who whuffled eagerly at the sight of her. "Good morning, Countess. Isn't it a lovely day?"

She stood stroking the mare's dark nose and watched Cal finish with the gelding.

A few minutes later he turned. "All set. Just let me pick up the saddlebags."

"Saddlebags?" Melinda asked, hearing the uneasiness creep into her voice and hating it.

"Just a little lunch," he said over his shoulder, busying himself with the task at hand. "With no breakfast and such an early start, I thought it might be a good idea."

For a moment Melinda hesitated. Lunch meant being away from the ranch for a long time.

"I've got an itinerary planned," Cal said. "I want you to see some of the country Russell loved." He had finished tying the saddlebags and turned to her. "All set."

"Great." She let the enthusiasm she was feeling come back into her voice. It was a beautiful morning and she wasn't going to spoil it by any stupid speculations about Cal. After all, here she was in Charlie Russell country! The thing to do was to learn all she could.

The sun was already bright as they led the horses out

into the stable yard and Melinda breathed in with delight. "You've no idea how good Montana's air smells after all those years in Chicago," she said.

Cal grinned. "I can imagine. Here, let me give you a leg up." He cupped his hands and held them for her.

Melinda gave him a grateful look. She hadn't been on a horse since she was ten and she wasn't at all sure that she could negotiate the intricacies of mounting by herself.

She took the saddle horn in her left hand and, putting her right on his shoulder to steady herself, stepped into his cupped palms and swung up into the saddle. It creaked beneath her weight and she smiled at this sound out of the past.

"How are the stirrups?" he asked.

Melinda raised herself and tested them. "They feel good."

He nodded. "I thought they'd be about right." Reins in hand, he swung up on Jericho's back with practiced ease, the long lean length of him fitting easily into the saddle. He looked so like the cowboy in the painting that Melinda heard herself asking, "Do you look like your father?"

He clucked to the horse and it began to move toward the gate and the prairie that lay beyond. Melinda's horse followed. "Yes. How did you know?"

"I was thinking of that painting," she admitted. "'When Branding Comes Round.' When I first saw it, I thought how much that cowboy looked like you. But I knew it couldn't have been you. Then, I heard how it was a present to your father and how much he valued it. And just now, seeing you on the horse, I realized it must be your father in the painting."

Cal nodded. "You're right," he said. "Dad loved ranch work. Did it whenever he could."

There was a long silence while Melinda wondered if he should ask about his parents. Then the lines around his mouth hardened and he said, "I lost them both shortly after Stephen's death. Mom had a heart attack and Dad followed her the next year."

"Oh." The word was a muted syllable of compassion. "I'm sorry."

"Those things can't be helped," he said, straightening his shoulders. "But that's enough of that." He gave her a smile. It wasn't quite up to par, but his expression had lightened. "Now for Charlie Russell country. You'll love it."

By the time the sun was high Melinda had seen a great deal of the country. She was also realizing that so many years out of the saddle had not prepared her for a long morning's ride. From time to time she shifted uneasily, trying to distribute her weight to a different portion of her anatomy, one that didn't ache. But that grew increasingly difficult as the ache spread.

If Cal noticed her discomfort, he wisely refrained from mentioning it. But he had a great deal to say about the country they were traversing, a long stretch of rolling prairie with a wash to one side.

Melinda had been listening eagerly, but now the protests of her body were beginning to override all other considerations. She was about to put aside her pride and admit to her problem when Cal reined Jericho to a halt. "Maybe you'd like to get down and walk a little."

"If I can," she replied ruefully. "I'm feeling pretty sore."

Cal grinned. "No doubt. There's a line shack over there." He gestured ahead of them where she could barely make out a weather-beaten shack huddled in a clump of cottonwoods.

The cottonwoods meant water, Melinda knew. Right now the idea of water was especially appealing. Except that she could hardly *sit* in it as she would really like to.

She followed him across the flower-dotted prairie into the shade of the trees. He swung down with an easy grace that she instantly envied. No sore, aching bottom for him!

He turned to her, a quizzical look on his face. "Need some help getting down?"

Her smile was forced. "'Fraid so." Gingerly she swung one foot over the front of the saddle. Then his hands were around her waist, lifting her away from the saddle so that she slid to the ground in one smooth motion, not touching anything on the way down.

She breathed a sigh of deep relief. "Thank you. I wonder if I can walk."

His arm was around her, strong and supportive. "Take it easy. I'll help. Let's go over by the stream and sit—"

He stopped. When she began to laugh, he joined her. "I think maybe I'll stand," she said when she was able to talk again. "If you don't mind."

"I don't mind. I'd carry you, except that the walking is good for you. It helps to iron out the kinks."

She shook her head. "I don't think I'll ever be the same again. When I was little, why, I used to ride for hours on end. I never thought—"

"It's different when you're a child," he said. "Your body is tougher. Now your body is softer."

For the first time since they'd stopped she was completely aware of his closeness. The aching and soreness retreated from her consciousness, leaving her breathtakingly aware of his physical nearness.

"I—I think I'm all right now," she stammered.

But he didn't release her waist. "It's not much further. Better let me help you."

Wordlessly she let him walk her along, the sod cushioning their steps. She hadn't the strength to pull away from him. Besides, that would reveal all too clearly the thoughts that were going through her chaotic mind, thoughts of being in his arms, thoughts of kissing him, thoughts of—

"Here we are," he said, helping her through the trees. "Do you want to lie down?"

She shook her head and eyed the stream wistfully. "I'd really like just to sit in that."

"It'd be awfully cold."

"Good. That might numb the aching."

His eyes searched hers. "We can if you want to."

"Can what?" His remark took her by surprise.

"We can go swimming."

"I haven't any suit."

"Neither have I."

Her breath caught in her throat as his black eyes bored into hers.

"That doesn't matter. No one will see us out here."

"But—but we'll see each other."

"You're forgetting. You don't find me attractive." His eyes mocked her.

"I didn't say that—I—" She realized she had given herself away.

"Oh?" He turned her to face him, his hands light on her waist.

She felt she should move away from him, but her feet refused to budge. Her heart was pounding in her throat. "I said—That is—"

"You said you didn't know me." His eyes were smoldering and his hands seemed to burn into her waist.

"I—yes. That's what I said." She couldn't take her eyes away from his. Longing rose up inside her, longing so urgent that she felt it as an actual hurt.

His hands slid around her, pulling her closer. "Do you know me now?"

It was a loaded question. Desire pulsed through her and she clenched her fists to keep herself from touching him. Her lips seemed suddenly dry; she moistened them with the tip of her tongue. "Of course, but—"

He didn't let her finish. His mouth came down on hers, slowly enough that she could have twisted away, but fast enough so that she didn't have too much time to think about it.

She didn't try to avoid it. She was incapable of that. After all, her body had been clamoring for his touch for the last week. It was a long kiss. Like a symphony, it was composed of several movements. The first touch of his lips was tentative, almost fearful, but when she didn't pull away, when her hands crept up to his shoulders and then moved around behind his neck, he drew her closer still and increased the pressure.

In some dim recess of her mind she thought she should fight him. This was not the cowboy Cal, not someone she could ever envision herself sharing a future with. And she had promised herself that there would be no more Tom Ryders in her life.

But there was no fight in her. Her whole body molded itself to his; it fit perfectly, as though they had been made for each other. Her lips softened beneath his, softened and opened.

His hands moved up her back, crushing her against him and she welcomed it. If only there were some way to get closer still, she thought, as his tongue mingled with hers. Another surge of desire swept through her and she felt her knees begin to sag. If he let go of her now, she would fall right at his feet. There was no strength left in her bones.

From tenderness and persuasion, his kiss moved to passion, and carried her with it. His lips were hard, demanding, bruising hers in their need. But she didn't care. Her need was as great as his. She would give him anything, anything he wanted.

And then he put her from him. "I'm sorry," he said

ruefully. "I meant to approach this more gradually. But I couldn't wait."

Melinda tried to think straight. Her mind was still a mad whirl of thoughts and her body didn't want to leave the touch of his. "I—don't understand."

He kissed her forehead. "I've wanted you so much. All week long, thinking about it every time I saw you." He shook his head. "Sometimes I didn't think I could hold out. But I wanted to let you get to know me. To know Colin Marsden as well as Cal." He smiled down at her. "And last night—at bedtime—you'll never know how hard it was for me to walk away from you."

"I still don't understand." She fought an impusle to reach up and kiss his chin.

"Please, Melinda. Forget the bad first impression you had of me. You know me better now. Let me show you who I really am."

"But—" She tried to summon all the reasons she had for not giving in to him, but they all seemed to have vanished. "You're Colin Marsden. You're an important man."

He sighed. "A lonely man," he returned. "You can't know what it's like to be wanted for your money. Never to be sure if people care about *you.*" His hand moved on her back, softly caressing. "That's why I started to go around as Cal. It worked at the Halfway House. I thought it might work other places. I need to be accepted as a person. It's not that I'm trying to deceive anyone, only that I need to be accepted as a human being, not as an 'important man.' Can you understand that?"

"I think so. But—"

"Please, Melinda. I need you. I admit, at first you were a challenge to me. Not many women walk away from me. Not even when I'm Cal."

He said this simply, as if stating a fact. She nodded.

"But as I got to know you, it grew to be more than that.

We share a love of the West, of art. I want to share another important part of myself with you. Share it in a way I never have before."

She shook her head. "I need to think." This could be just another line, the voice in her head was saying. A new line, very effective even, but just a line.

"I don't mean to push you," he said, slipping an arm around her waist. "Would you like to see the inside of the line shack? There might be some furnishings still there. Dad and Charlie Russell used to stop here sometimes."

"Yes. I want to see it."

As he led her toward the shack, his arm still around her, she tried to think clearly. He was asking her to sleep with him, to share a part of him. He was asking her for a gift of herself. But she didn't know how to handle this. Tom Ryder hadn't given her any time to think. His mouth and his hands had been so busy that first time that she'd been swept completely away.

She knew that if Cal had taken that approach, had kissed her till she was breathless and then carried her into the line shack, she wouldn't have resisted him. Not this time.

But this was so different. So cold-blooded. Yet so fair, said another voice in her head. This time the decision was hers. There would be no one to blame afterwards. No way to say he'd seduced her, he'd overcome her resistance. If she told him yes, she would have to take the responsibility on herself.

Was she willing to do that? Was she willing to give herself in a one-time act? He hadn't said that, of course; but it could very well be only once. And how would she deal with that afterwards? But then, how would she deal with the knowledge that she could have shared something wonderful with him and had refused because of her fear, because of Tom Ryder and what he had done to her?

Cal opened the door to the shack. "Looks like it's still stocked. We keep some stuff in all the old shacks. In case somebody gets stuck in bad weather. Many times it turns out real handy."

She looked around her. The inside of the shack was almost as weather-beaten as the outside and its furnishings were old and battered. A scarred table, a couple of chairs, several bunks built into the wall, a small round stove with a pile of wood beside it and a box of matches prominently displayed. She could have stepped back into the past, right back into Charlie Russell's times.

The air was cool and slightly musty after the freshness of the prairie, and cobwebs festooned the ceilings and walls. She longed for the openness they had just left. "I'm glad I saw it," she said. "But could we go back outside?"

"Of course." His tone was evenly polite and he didn't question her decision. "Shall we go down by the creek?"

"Yes."

She had regained the strength in her legs now, but she didn't move away from his encircling arm. It was good being close to him, good feeling the solidity of his muscled side against her.

At the edge of the little creek he stopped. The water was crystal clear. Melinda gazed at it in awe. "It looks so pure."

"It probably is. Here, here's a grassy bank. Maybe you can sit down."

His words brought back to her consciousness the ache in her limbs, but now it didn't seem to matter.

He helped her settle herself on the thick sod and then dropped down beside her, his arm around her. The pungent smell of sage and mesquite hung in the air. For a long moment he looked into her eyes and her blood began to quicken. Then he bent his head and claimed her lips again, pulling her backward with him so that she lay against his side and not on her back.

"Is that comfortable?" he asked as he released her lips.

"Yes." The word was only a whisper. Are you going to let your fear keep you from doing what you really want to? asked a persistent voice in her head. Are you going to let Tom Ryder mess up your life again?

His hand moved to the front of her shirt, cupped the swell of her breast pushing against the plaid, and he sighed deeply. "God, how I want you." But he made no further move, didn't try to put his hand inside her shirt.

"Help me, Melinda. Tell me what to do." His voice was low and husky. "Shall I stop? Or will you share yourself with me?"

The two voices inside her head warred with each other, but Melinda ignored them. Tom Ryder wasn't going to cheat her out of this. Cal wanted her. He wanted her quite simply as the woman she really was. And she wanted him, wanted Cal the cowboy and Colin the art connoiseur.

She drew a deep breath. "I don't want you to stop," she whispered. "I want to share myself with you."

He kissed her again. Softly, gently. "I'm glad," came the whisper beside her ear. "Do you want to go into the shack?" There was a pause as he unbuttoned her shirt. "Or we could stay here."

"Here?" she replied. "But someone might come."

"No, love. The prairie's all ours. And this little grove. No one's likely to come around here. It's too isolated."

"I—" The idea of being out in the open appealed to her. It made the moment lovelier. "Here," she whispered. "Let's make love here."

"All right." He had finished unbuttoning her shirt. His fingers moved across the bare skin above her bra. She sighed. She wanted to be close to him. To feel the whole length of him against her. He pulled off her shirt, unhooked her bra, let her clothing fall in a pile on the grass. Gently, reverently, he touched her breasts. Then he bent and kissed them, first one, then the other.

Desire pulsed through her as he laid her carefully on her back, his fingers reaching for his own shirt. His chest was well muscled, as she had known it would be, and darkly tanned, fine golden fuzz highlighted against it. Reaching up, she ran a tentative finger down it, relishing the sensation against her sensitive fingertips.

He smiled, a tender amused smile, and turned his back on her. "Give me your foot."

She did so, wondering what he was doing.

"Put your other boot on my back."

"But I'll hurt you!"

"Nonsense. Brace your other foot on my back. This is the best way to take off boots."

Obediently she did as he said. He pulled off one boot, then the other, then turned to her with a sheepish grin. "Maybe you'd better take off your jeans yourself. I wouldn't want to hurt you."

She nodded and sat up, her hands moving to her belt. Her aches and pains seemed to have vanished. She was not embarrassed by undressing in front of him. He wanted her body and that made it beautiful. But she couldn't help looking at him. At his long legs, covered with a light fuzz, at his hard flat stomach, at the rest of him.

He put his clothes to one side and dropped down beside her. "Now," he said. "Now, sweetheart. . . ."

His hand moved up to stroke her shoulder, to caress her neck and the sensitive skin behind her ear. She felt her breath quicken. She could feel her breasts pressed against his chest. To her surprise she discovered that her hand had moved of its own will and was gliding softly over his side. She felt the tightening of his arm around her, almost as though he feared she would move away.

And then the hand that had caressed her neck stole beneath her chin and cupped it. For a long moment they lay in complete silence. And then he began slowly and inexorably to tilt back her head.

She shut her eyes as his face came in view, her lashes dark against her cheeks.

"Melinda." His voice was a caress of silk. "Look at me, love."

The last word brought her eyes open in a hurry to find that his were only inches away. They gleamed in the sunlight.

"Melinda," he said again, his voice gone hoarse with passion. "God, how I've wanted to do this." And his lips met hers.

It was a gentle kiss, slow and persuasive, and it sent shivers of delight over her body. The pressure of his mouth was gentle, but it was persistent and under it her lips opened and softened.

Melinda had known passion before. Tom Ryder had been an experienced seducer, wise enough to see that his women got enough satisfaction to keep them coming back, but there was a difference here. It was as though, all unwittingly, she had kept something from Tom, some part of herself still inviolate. But now she felt herself opening up, not waiting for it to be taken, but offering this secret part of herself, freely and joyously, to the man who held her.

His mouth left hers finally to slide in little nibbling kisses across her throat and up to her ear. He was breathing heavily as his tongue outlined the lobe of her ear and a shiver of desire went over her. She felt the prickling of the grass against her bare skin, smelled the warm earth beneath them.

Then he was rolling away from her, just enough to free one breast for his hand. His seeking fingers found the rosy peak, already half-erect, and caressed it gently. A soft moan came from her partly open mouth as she felt another shiver of pleasure quiver over her. Round and round, he trailed his fingers on the velvet-soft flesh and she could almost feel it rising up to meet his caressing hand. He raised himself on one elbow and trailed a row of wet kisses down her throat to the soft mound, then let his tongue replace his fingers.

Melinda's breath came in soft pants as her body arched up against his caressing tongue. She longed for him in a way she had never longed for Ryder, but she knew instinctively that Cal would take his time. He would want this to be as good for her as it was for him.

His mouth moved to her other breast and Melinda sighed as his tongue worked there. And then his seeking hand moved slowly, tentatively, across the smooth flatness of her stomach and beyond.

Her soft moans came more rapidly now and she clutched at the hard shoulder near her. Then his shoulder slid out of her grasp and again his mouth followed his hand, down the smoothness of her stomach and raining little kisses on the tender flesh of her thighs.

Melinda sighed in pure bliss. She knew with an overwhelming certainty that she wanted this man, wanted him with every passionate cell in her yearning body.

And still he did not finish, but used his hands and mouth to raise her to even greater heights. She lay twisting beneath his restraining arm, her breath coming in short quick gasps.

"Please, Cal. Oh please!" The plea was torn from her.

He released the pressure of his hands on her legs and turned to kneel over her. Her hands clutched at his hard shoulders as she tried to lift herself toward him, to taste again the sweetness of his mouth. Her breasts grazed the hair on his chest as she wrapped her arms around his neck and tried to pull him down on top of her. If she did not soon feel the wonderful weight of him on her, she would explode.

But, although he put his arms around her and held her so, he refused to be pulled down. He kissed her nose, her eyes, her chin, in quick succession, and then his lips settled on her mouth.

To the very depths of her soul that kiss jarred her. It called forth from her an even greater urgency to feel the long hard length of him against her, and her hands dug into his back in her efforts to pull him down. But she did not succeed.

Then suddenly she found her face against the curling hair of his chest and she kissed the warm flesh, her tongue flicking out to lightly touch his nipples. He rolled on his back beside her, a groan of ecstasy coming from his lips.

Then Melinda understood. This was to be mutual giving and taking. Cal wanted to be kissed and caressed too. As she moved to her knees beside him and her tongue flicked over his stomach in a quick path, she was glad, for the first time in many months, for her experience with Tom. She knew what pleased a man and she wanted to please this big man lying so quietly beside her, letting her have the initiative in their lovemaking.

She let her hand trail softly up his leg, the hair fine under her questing fingers. Her tongue followed and Cal's body twitched with the force of his feeling. She felt a thrill at being able to give pleasure to the man who had given her so much.

Then suddenly he sat up and with strong hands laid her on her back. The feel of him was so sweet that she cried out at the joy of it, at the wonderful weight of his body against her.

"Now?" he murmured hoarsely.

And her answer came quickly. "Yes, oh yes, Cal."

He raised himself on his elbows and looked down at her for a moment and then he was entering her. She sighed in contentment at the good masculine feel of him and she scattered little kisses across the shoulder nearest her mouth as he buried his face in her neck.

"Oh God," he muttered. "So good." And she clutched at him, feeling she could never get him quite close enough to her yearning flesh.

And still he was slow and easy, bringing her several times to the edge of ecstasy before they both tumbled over in a paroxysm of pleasure.

His weight was heavy on her, but she liked it. In some strange fashion it meant security. She wished to keep him there, forever, safe within her arms.

She sighed when he rolled off her, but he gathered her quickly against his side. "Don't worry," he said with the faintest of grins. "I won't roll over and fall asleep."

Melinda flushed, wondering how he could know that Tom had always done that particular thing to her, leaving her feeling bereft at the moment she should have felt safest.

Cal chuckled. "Don't look so shocked," he said easily. "A great many men do that. I never could understand why. I think the intimacy afterwards is one of the best parts."

Melinda, snuggling down against his side, could only agree, and uttered a deep sigh of contentment. A thought crept into her mind and was voiced before she considered. "Maybe some people are afraid to be that involved. Sex," she colored slightly, "can be very impersonal, almost mechanical." She was thinking of Ryder as she spoke. "I shouldn't think that people who are just using someone as a convenient 'object,' so to speak, would value the after part at all. They probably wouldn't see any sense to it. Since they already have what they were after."

He was eyeing her strangely and her flush deepened. "It's just an idea that occurred to me this minute," she said. "So I haven't given it much thought."

"Sounds plausible to me," Cal said, his fingers making lazy circles on her bare arm. "I hope you dumped that clown."

Melinda stiffened. "What are you talking about?" she demanded.

"About the clown who didn't value intimacy with you, the one who was a user."

"I never said—" Melinda's eyes widened with dismay.

"Didn't need to, honey. Your face gives you away. Anyhow, he wasn't just a clown, he was outright stupid. Not to know what a good thing he had."

Melinda felt a little chill of apprehension. This conversation was certainly strange. Wasn't Cal himself a user? Though she had to admit that he gave plenty in return.

"You know," Cal said thoughtfully, "even strangers can appreciate this kind of intimacy."

"They can?" She could not control the slight quaver in her voice and she did not raise her head to look at him.

"Sure. You can reveal yourself to another person even though you don't intend to be with him or her forever. There can be giving and taking."

"How is that different from using?" asked Melinda in a small voice.

"It's very different," said Cal, his breath soft against her forehead, "when you're concerned with the other person's pleasure, too. Users, you know, ordinarily think only of themselves."

Melinda sighed. Warm and contented in the crook of his arm, she was fast losing all her preconceived notions about the rich Colin Marsden. But she was still sane enough to see that it was quite dangerous to be with him. More dangerous, in fact, now that she had discovered the cold arrogant Colin hid the warm and tender man she first knew as Cal. For the hundredth time in the last week Melinda wished that he *was* the itinerant cowboy she had first imagined him. Things would have been so much simpler then.

She took a deep breath. "Hadn't we better get started back?" she said. "Your guests will worry."

For an instant she felt his body stiffen, then it relaxed again as he pulled her closer still against him. "No, they won't. They've been on their own lots of times. They won't even miss us."

"Still—" Melinda shifted the leg that lay across his.

That was all she did, for his hands were instantly on her hips, pulling her playfully on top of him. "Not yet," he said, "there's still plenty of time."

One arm around her waist kept her body tightly pressed against his. His other hand settled on the nape of her neck. A shiver of desire whispered down her spine at the touch of it. Then he was pulling her head down toward him until her mouth was only an inch from his. "Kiss me, woman," he said softly, and, exerting the last bit of necessary pressure, he pulled her mouth to his.

This was a new situation for Melinda. Tom had always assumed the initiative in their lovemaking. Now she was the one who could tease, pursue and withdraw, scatter little nibbling kisses over his face, take little bites at his ears.

When he was sure she did not intend to get up, he let his hands fall away from her waist, giving her the freedom to move around on his supine body. Sweet surges of joy flashed through her at the touching of her flesh and his. Softly, against his neck, she laughed. It was the sound of pure joy.

His arms tightened around her forcefully once more

and his lips found her ear. "And what is so funny?" he demanded in a tone of mock severity.

She wished she could get closer still. "Nothing," she replied. "Everything! Oh, I don't know. I just feel like laughing."

His arms squeezed her tighter. "Me, too," he said. "And now it's my turn." And with one thrust of his powerful body he rolled them both over and pinned her beneath him.

"No fair," she protested, but her voice gave no indication of regret.

He kissed the tip of her nose. "Listen, woman, don't get too big for your britches. I'm the man around here. You'd better remember it."

Melinda giggled. With the weight of his body on hers, his hard maleness pressing against her—"How *could* I forget?" she said, another laugh bubbling out of her throat. "With you like this?"

"Quiet, woman," he said sternly and Melinda giggled again.

This his lips descended on hers and he began to kiss her in earnest. Somewhat to her surprise, she felt him coming to her again. Tom had never desired her a second time so soon and she had supposed that what she and Cal were engaged in was a delightful kind of afterplay. Now that she recognized that it was not, she experienced a great surge of desire and her tongue darted out to mingle with his. For the first time it tentatively invaded his mouth. She felt the reaction in the hard body atop her own.

This time he did not take so long to arouse her to a fever pitch of desire. She wanted him as badly as he wanted her and her hands and mouth moved as passionately as his. And this time the sweet crescendo of their passion was even greater and she lay panting beneath him, her body quivering in ecstacy.

Again they lay quietly, their bodies intertwined, and the first time he moved to roll off her she clutched compulsively at his shoulders, drawing him closer against her. "Not yet," she pleaded, anxious to keep the feel of him as long as possible.

Obedient to her wishes, he lowered his weight on her again and she sighed in contentment. They lay for a few minutes longer and when he moved the second time she made no protest. It was time to face reality. Their fairy-tale afternoon was over and Melinda felt a heavy disappointment creeping over her.

Cal glanced at the watch on his wrist and sighed. "Sorry to say this, but we've got to get headed back. It'll take us a while. And we don't want to spend the night on the prairie. It wouldn't be as cozy then."

Melinda nodded. Suddenly shy, she rolled away. Cal's big hand stopped her. "One hug to hold me till tonight. Okay?"

He had her in his arms again before Melinda had a chance to protest. But she would not have in any case for her mind was busy considering his words—"till tonight" he had said. She felt a surge of joy; it was tinged with sadness, of course. For tomorrow they would return to Helena and what was between them would be over. Here at the ranch it was easy to forget Helena and Colin Marsden, to think only of the cowboy Cal. But back there it would be different. In the Marsden Mansion she was an interloper, an art teacher who would soon be gone.

As Cal released her, she shut the thought of the future away. They would have tonight, at least. And he was right. Two strangers could reach a high level of intimacy. She rose to her feet and moved toward her clothes.

With a slight feeling of embarrassment she turned her back to him as she dressed. It was one thing to lie naked beside him, it was quite another to go parading around like that in front of the man.

She turned just as he was pulling on his boots. His shirt was unbuttoned almost to his waist and she longed to move close to him and rest her head against his chest. She steeled herself not to do it. These feelings of tenderness were caused by the intimacy they had experienced, not only of bodies but of souls. It was a perfectly normal reaction, she told herself sternly, especially given the already strong attraction between them. And anyway it was good to know how it would be with another man, to realize that they weren't all like Tom.

"Hungry now?" he asked, turning a smile her way.

She shook her head. "Couldn't we eat when we get back?"

He shrugged. "'Spose so, but it'll be dark."

"All the more reason to get started now," said Melinda earnestly. For some reason she could not bear the thought of eating here. It seemed so normal and mundane after the enchantment she had experienced.

"All set?" he asked.

Picking up her Stetson, Melinda nodded. "Yes."

He shouldered the saddlebags and she followed him to the horses without looking around. The whole area was imprinted on her memory; she had no need to look at it to remember.

Jericho whickered as they approached and stretched his neck toward them.

"Hello, old fellow." Cal patted his nose.

Melinda turned to the mare and winced.

"We could ride double. Lead the mare."

"But—" Melinda stared at him. "Won't that take longer? They'll be really worried."

He shook his head. "No." He threw the saddlebags on Countess and tied them fast, then swung easily up on Jericho.

Melinda felt a thrill of pride as she watched him. This wonderful-looking man had wanted her; he still did.

"Want to ride in front or in back?" he asked, grinning down at her.

She groaned. "I guess it doesn't matter. It's going to be gruesome either way."

His grin broadened. "You seemed agile enough a while ago."

Melinda glared at him with mock anger. "I wasn't using quite the same muscles.

"Let's try the front," she finally decided. She took the strong hand he extended her, set her boot on the toe of his, and swung up. He caught her as she came and helped her to a position in front of him. Melinda bit back a groan as her bottom hit the saddle.

"Easy does it," he said. "We'll be going in slow stages. Sometimes I can shift you around sideways. Across my legs."

Melinda looked at him over her shoulder. She remembered quite vividly how she had clung to him out there on the prairie. Just being this near to him was already making her wish they were back there.

As Jericho moved off across the prairie and the mare followed, Melinda felt a strong arm go round her waist and pull her tight against him. "Relax," he whispered against her ear. "I'll get you there in one piece. I promise."

10

~~~~~~~~~~~~~

Forever after that, Melinda would remember that afternoon as a jumble of mixed emotions. She tried to focus her mind on the scenery around her. She might not get to see Charlie Russell country again. But her body was aware only of the man behind her, the feel of his warm chest against her back, the whisper of his breath against her ear, the strength of his arm around her waist.

As Jericho turned up the lane to the ranch house the sun was falling below the horizon. It was a spectacular sunset and part of Melinda's mind recognized that. But the rest of it was busy wondering what kind of excuse Cal would offer for their lateness and whether or not Ruth Farmwood's eyes would narrow shrewdly as she looked at them. She was so busy considering this that they were almost up to the house before she realized that only one car, Cal's battered station wagon, stood in the ranch yard.

As the horses halted at the stable door, Melinda glanced over her shoulder at Cal. "Where is everyone? Could they be out looking for us?"

"No." His eyes seemed to suddenly cloud over. Taking

his arm from around her, he swung lightly down, then reached up for her.

She did not resist the hands that spanned her waist and she did not try to escape them after he set her on her feet. "How can you be so sure?"

Her hands had moved automatically to his chest. By this time it seemed natural to be always in physical contact with him. Under her fingers she felt his heart thud harder and his face settled into strange lines, so that for a moment he seemed like the coldly arrogant Colin Marsden and not the warm, affectionate man she had come to know today.

Then he grinned. It seemed a little artificial, but she did not give it much thought at that moment. "They went home this morning," he said.

"Home?" For a minute Melinda could only stare at him. "Why?"

"That seems fairly obvious."

She was sure now that his grin was strained.

"So we could be alone," he continued.

She twisted sharply to free herself from his hands on her waist, but they tightened automatically. "You set the whole thing up! You—you planned it!" She glared up at him. "All that smooth talk about the experts wanting to meet me!"

"They did," he said calmly. "You know they enjoyed last night. So did you."

Melinda did know this, but her anger was roused now. "You lied to me," she cried. "You deliberately lied to me!"

He shook his head. "I didn't say how long they'd stay. Only that they'd be here."

"It's the same thing. You didn't tell me all the truth." He was like Ryder, she told herself, with the same slick way of getting what he wanted.

"I wanted to be alone with you," he replied, his voice solemn. "I wanted the joy I glimpsed that night up on Mt. Helena. I thought maybe here you'd give it to me. You had a bad impression of me. I wanted a chance to change it."

How his ego must have been hurt, she told herself bitterly, to go to all this trouble. But of course he had to do it. A man with all those women after him couldn't stand thinking that one had refused him.

"Let me go!" She was fuming now, and he saw it, letting his hands fall away from her.

"You set it all up," she cried. "You would have had me one way or another! All that fancy talk out on the prairie! It meant nothing, nothing at all!" She turned toward the house.

Strong hands on her shoulders stopped her before she reached the veranda. "Melinda." He swung her around. "Do you really think I would take you against your will?"

Honesty compelled her to voice a small "No."

He stared down at her, his dark eyes searching her face. "This week I gave you a chance to know me. I was carefully polite. I refrained from even touching you. I let you know me as Colin Marsden. And out here I let you know me as Cal."

"You certainly went to a lot of trouble." Anger was bitter in her mouth. He couldn't stand to have his masculinity insulted. She had been mistaken, she thought fiercely. He wasn't different from Ryder. He was smoother, but he was still a user.

"Will you take me back to Helena now?" She put the question to him squarely.

His answer was just as direct. "No. The weekend isn't over yet."

"It is as far as I'm concerned." And the look she gave him left little doubt of what she meant. Just to be sure, she continued. "I'm glad to know you would never take a woman by force," she said nastily. "That should mean I'm safe."

For a moment he looked as though he would shake her, and then he sighed deeply. "Maybe it's just hunger that's making you so crabby. As soon as I call someone to take care of the horses, I'd better fix us something to eat." He dropped his hands from her shoulders.

Melinda considered refusing the meal, but she was suddenly ravenously hungry. She sent a glance toward the battered station wagon, but she distinctly remembered him taking the keys from the ignition the night before. And besides, even if she could get it started, she would only get herself lost. She felt stupid enough as it was, letting him trick her like that. Falling into his hands like a ripe apple! Red flooded her cheeks as she trudged up the steps.

"Why don't you go take a nice shower?" Cal said, his voice politely even. "I'll start the grub and grab a quick one myself. Meet you in the kitchen."

Melinda's nod was curt. She was still angry and she meant to hold on to that rage. After all, she wasn't responsible for the state of Colin Marsden's ego. He was just another conniving male, out to prove his masculinity. Well, he wasn't going to get any more proof from her!

She shut the bedroom door behind her with a decided thud and threw herself down on the bed. She yanked at her boots and cursed as her memory presented her with a picture of Cal's back as he bent to remove them that afternoon. Irritably, Melinda dropped the boots on the floor and stripped off her clothes. Then she turned the shower on full blast and stepped under it.

When she emerged some minutes later, every square inch of her had been scrubbed and rescrubbed, but she could not wash away the feel of Cal's body. She shampooed her hair and towelled it vigorously dry, wishing she had never heard of Colin Marsden.

Angrily she slipped into clean clothes. She debated about putting her boots back on; she wanted nothing that came from that man. But common sense won out and she shoved her stockinged feet back into them with a violence that testified to her still raging anger. Part of it, of course, was directed at herself. She should have known better than to come out here with him. Should have known the man couldn't be trusted. She stuffed her shirt angrily into her jeans, ran a brush through her damp hair, and left the room, barely refraining from slamming the door behind her.

The kitchen was empty when she reached it, a pot of stew simmering on the stove. She couldn't stop herself from sniffing appreciatively. Her stomach felt like a bottomless pit.

She opened various cupboard doors until she found the dishes and silver to set the big oak table. She would remain calm and polite, but that was all. Certainly she did not intend to share his bed again. She had been taken in by Tom Ryder, but she had thought she'd learned her lesson. And now to realize that the same thing had happened again— The thought infuriated her.

A footstep behind her made her whirl suddenly. Cal stood in the doorway. He had showered—his pale hair still glistened with dampness—and changed his jeans and shirt. He had not finished buttoning his shirt yet and the fine hair on his chest was plainly visible. Melinda's body reacted automatically and she barely stopped her hand from reaching out to him.

He smiled at her as though nothing had gone wrong. "Thanks for setting the table. That'll speed things up."

"You're welcome." Melinda made her reply as cool as possible, but when he nonchalantly unbuckled his belt in preparation to tucking in his shirt, she turned rather too hastily back toward the sink. It would be better to make him think he had no effect on her, she knew. It was a little late for that, though, said a sharp voice within her. After this afternoon he wasn't likely to believe anything like that. No, she had made a complete fool of herself, playing right into his hands.

He chose not to make anything of her turning away, but finished tucking in his shirt and gave his attention to the stew. "Looks like it's hot enough," he said conversationally. "I'll dish it up. There's milk in the refrigerator. Will you pour some?"

"Yes." In the face of his calmness Melinda felt a little ridiculous. Obviously she couldn't go about ranting and raging all evening. Not when he was behaving like this. She decided a cool politeness was called for.

The meal was not a comfortable one. She knew Cal was making every effort to get her to relax, to bring back the easy camaraderie of their afternoon together. But Melinda did not give in. Her anger, though it had not seemed to bother him, had had the effect of releasing her from his spell. She was no longer lulled by the feel of his body into a mood where reason had little chance to prevail. No, she was wide awake now, wide awake and coldly analytical.

And the truth was easy enough to see. The afternoon had been a mistake—a bad mistake. She was not the woman for a short-term affair. She had never indulged in one-night stands; they had never made any sense to her. The best thing to do was to stop this right now. She shivered slightly. It would take her a long time to wipe the memories of this afternoon from her mind—and from her senses. But she would do it.

And it was far better to begin now. This afternoon should never have happened. She would act as though it hadn't and go on from there. One or two more days work with the collection and she could leave Helena, put all this behind her—forever.

She finished up her stew and drained her glass of milk. "I was hungry," she said politely. "That was good."

"Thank you." His tone was even, but his eyes were dancing.

"Now I'm tired. I'm going to bed."

"Good night."

He said the words so calmly that she stared at him suspiciously. She couldn't imagine him giving in so easily.

"Sleep well," he said, apparently oblivious to her expression.

"I intend to." Anger gave her statement more force than she had meant it to convey, but still he did not respond, just turned to the stove and ladled himself another bowl of stew.

"I'll clean up the kitchen before I come up."

Melinda clamped her lips together over the harsh retort she'd been about to make. Let him think what he liked. Once she was in that room she meant to lock the door—and keep it locked!

No more words were exchanged between them and Melinda made her way up the stairs slowly. It had been a long difficult day, she told herself, and she was tired.

She closed the door to the room behind her and turned the key in the lock. There, that was done. Let him try to get in now. The sheer male affrontery of it—to go to so much effort when he knew that in a few weeks—or more likely a few days—it would all be over. He would be tired of her. Well, as far as she was concerned, it was already over. And it was going to stay that way.

Wearily she undressed, automatically laying her clothes out neatly. The filmy nightgown—a leftover from her early days with Ryder—slid sensously over her skin. Melinda cursed softly. Would her body always be like this? Always remembering the touch of Cal's hands and mouth, yearning for the feel of him, for the security of his weight on her.

With a muffled groan Melinda turned toward the bed. To sleep naked would be even worse. She climbed in and pulled the covers up to her chin.

Ten minutes later she realized that she had not moved, that she was lying there clutching the covers with hands that trembled. And then there came the sound of his footsteps on the stairs and she knew what she'd been waiting for. The footsteps approached her door and stopped. She heart the slight rattle as he tried the knob and found it locked. Shivering, she steeled herself—whether for persuasion or threats she did not know. And then the footsteps moved on; without a word he walked away.

For several minutes she couldn't believe it. Then gradually, as the minutes passed, she let herself relax. She had evidently convinced him. She sighed deeply. Now all she had to do was convince herself. Every cell in her body was longing for contact with his. It was going to be a long night, Melinda thought with resignation. A very long night.

11

≈≈≈≈≈≈≈≈≈≈

It was only a few moments later, however, when she heard the noise, the faintest sound of metal against metal. Her eyes went wildly to the window, but then common sense prevailed. This was the second floor, no one was coming in the window.

The door! He was doing something to the door. She clutched the covers and tried to think. Of course. She should have known he would have a key.

The soft sound of the lock turning reached her ears and she sat up quickly. The bed was no longer a place of refuge. Not with Colin Marsden outside that door! Frightened, she swung her legs over the edge of the bed and put her feet to the floor. The bare wood was cold and she grimaced silently as she crept across the room. She had left her suitcase by the window, the suitcase that held her robe.

The room was dark and she had to move slowly. She didn't dare put on the light. If he saw her like this— She had to get into her robe.

She was almost there when he opened the door. Then light flooded the room and she turned to gasp as he calmly entered the room. His smile was rather grim. "Hello, Melinda. Hope I didn't wake you."

"What—" She fought for coherence. "What are you doing here?"

His eyes gleamed dangerously as he let them slide down over her body, almost fully revealed by the flimsy nightgown. "That seems fairly obvious."

"But—" Melinda backed away as he strode into the room. "You promised— You said—" She stopped abruptly as she found herself up against a wall. She took a deep breath. "You said you've never forced a woman."

"I haven't," he replied. He was close now, so close she could smell the good male scent of him, so close she could feel the heat of his body.

She tried to move away, to sidle out from against the wall, but he was too quick for her. A brown hand went out on either side of her shoulders. Resting against the wall, they kept her effectively imprisoned. She shivered as those dark eyes looked down into hers.

"Don't worry, Melinda," he said softly. "I won't force you. You'll be willing."

"This—this is unfair." She tried to face him with dignity but she was pitifully aware of the scantiness of her attire. "I told you—I don't want to go to bed with you."

"Really?" His voice was dangerously soft and one hand moved over slightly to trace a tantalizing line down her throat.

"Don't do that!" she cried. "Don't—don't touch me."

"Why not, Melinda? What are you afraid of? Me? Or yourself?" His eyes came to rest on her breasts, fully revealed by the sheer chiffon.

"It's— You're being unfair," she repeated. "You said—"

One of his hands moved to the soft mound of a breast, tracing teasing circles round and round until she thought her legs would fail her.

"I know you want me," he said, his voice soft but deadly. "And I want you. I'm not going to let you ruin our weekend."

"I don't—" Melinda began, but the increasing pressure of his hand turned the words into a moan.

He pressed her against the wall, his hard body driving against hers. She felt the urgent rising of desire and a frantic need to feel his naked flesh against her own.

Still, she tried to twist her head sideways, to avoid the demanding mouth that was seeking her own. But he pinned her face between two hard calloused palms.

"You're not going to run away this time," he said. "I want the rest of this weekend, Melinda. I worked hard to get it." His eyes gazed deeply into hers. "How many times I held myself back when I wanted so desperately to take you in my arms, to kiss you."

Her lips quivered as she stared up at him. The hardness of his body pressed against her even more tightly and she felt the evidence of his need. Then his mouth descended.

She could not move her head, imprisoned as it was by his palms. Her own hands, though free, were entirely ineffective. She pulled at his arms, but they were immovable.

His mouth possessed hers. It was as though her body had been made especially for his, each individual nerve attuned to him. His mouth explored hers, tenderly, gently, seeking out its contours as his hand had previously sought her body's. His mouth was gentle, but his body was not. Hard and insistent, it flattened her against the wall, making plain its demands.

Melinda fought for breath—and sanity. The whole thing was crazy. Tomorrow the weekend would be over. Cal would have had his fun and where would she be?

But tomorrow's concerns grew less and less important as his mouth continued to hold hers. Her hands stopped pulling ineffectively at his arms and crept up to circle his neck. He was drawing all her strength out of her, threatening to reduce her to a pliant, helpless thing. But still she fought.

When he finally released her mouth, his lips slid down the sweet curve of her throat, down the top of her shoulder, then up again to the sensitive area behind her ear. She shivered uncontrollably and her hands pushed at him futilely.

"Please," she begged. "Go away. Leave me alone." The last was almost a whimper as his hands slid down her body and came to rest on her waist. She felt their heat through the sheer chiffon.

"You don't mean that," he replied, his voice dangerously soft. "You wanted me this afternoon and you want me now." His hands moved slowly against her bare midriff and she quivered with the intensity of her feelings.

"N-no. You—" She struggled to get the words out. "You said you never—force a woman."

He nodded, but his hands did not fall away from her waist.

"You—you're forcing me."

He shook his head. "I'm no teenage boy," he said. "I know when a woman wants me." His eyes gleamed. "But I'll make you a bargain."

She hardly dared breathe. Though his body no longer pinned hers to the wall, it was far too close for comfort. "What—is it?" She hated the way her voice broke, but she couldn't help herself.

"I'm a sporting man," he said. "If you can withstand my kiss, I'll back off. Leave you alone. But if you respond, then we'll do things my way."

Melinda tried to regain her dignity. She had never been one to give in to panic; she did not want to start now. But the feelings clashing inside her were so strong. She wanted him so badly that she had to clench her fists to keep from reaching out to touch the hard body so near her own.

"Do you agree?" he asked, his eyes dancing.

"That—hardly seems fair," she replied, trying to put coldness in her voice. "You got me out here by trickery and now you have the upper hand."

He shook his head in exasperation. "What a hypocrite you are," he said, one hand moving slowly up her side.

Trying to ignore his exploring fingers, she stared indignantly. "Hypocrite? Why?"

The harsh lines of his mouth softened into a half smile. "You're not stupid, Melinda. You must have been aware of the sexual tension between us—there in the gallery."

"I—I had to work on my book," she mumbled, knowing that she had sidestepped his question.

"But you *were* aware." His eyes insisted on an answer and finally she gave it.

"Yes."

"And knowing that you came out here."

"I thought— That is, I hoped—" She faltered, knowing that she dared not speak the truth. For she was only now realizing what she had actually been hoping for.

"I'm a man, Melinda." His voice was growing hoarse with passion. "And I want you. I've wanted you since that first moment I saw you on Deadwood's main street."

His hand reached her breast and a delicious shiver traveled down her backbone. She mustered all her strength. "I want to be left alone," she declared, striving for a firm tone.

"No you don't," he said, his lips against her ear. And as he spoke he moved his hand slightly, causing her nipple to rise up against his palm.

If only she could escape this room. She was beyond reason now, willing to face the darkness outside—for if she stayed here much longer, if he kissed her like that again— Her body burned at the thought. She wrenched herself violently sideways, but he was too quick for her, his arms sliding around her to gather her against him.

"Don't be foolish," he said softly. "You can't run out into the night like that." He reached to one side and shut off the hall light. "Come to bed, Melinda. You know you want to."

"You said—if I could withstand your kiss," she reminded him.

The moonlight made his eyes shine as he drew closer. "All right, Melinda." His body drew nearer hers. "Play your little game to the end."

"It isn't a game," she protested. How unfair of him. *He* was the one who saw all this as a game. For her it was deadly serious. She steeled herself to reject his kiss, to disregard her longing for the feel of his body. If only she could remain cold, could convince him that his kiss was meaningless. She bent all her concentration to the task, willing herself to ignore the feel of his body against hers.

She managed to maintain her coldness when his mouth met hers, when she felt her breasts crushed against his chest. She kept her lips firmly closed against the advances of his tongue. But when one hand moved slowly up her back to caress the nape of her neck and the other moved down to her hip to crowd their bodies closer still, she could not stifle the soft moan that escaped her mouth.

And then he had her. His seeking tongue explored the sweetness of her mouth with an intensity that left her legs feeling boneless. His arms pressed her closer still; the breath seemed squeezed from her helpless body. Her arms went around him, clinging fiercely to him, her body as demanding as his. Her fingers traced the hard muscles of his back, her lips returned his kisses, her tongue reached out to find his. Her whole body was aflame, she thought through a sensuous haze, aflame with an intense desire for him.

His arms lifted her easily from her feet. Still keeping her body tight against his own, he moved toward the bed. Gently, tenderly, he laid them down, their bodies separating only as he removed their clothing.

Her breath came in great gulps; she could not seem to get enough air into her lungs. Every cell in her body was achingly alive. She desired him with every fiber of her being. Her yearning body thrust upward against his, desiring him, needing him.

He buried his face in her throat, his breath hot against her ear. "Melinda." The word was a groan of passion. "I want you! God how I want you. Say you want me."

"I do." The words were a mere whisper.

"Say it louder," he begged. "Tell me."

"I do, Cal, I do." She was past caring now; she knew only that she needed him. She needed him *now*. That was the only reality in her life. This tremendous overwhelming need for him that erased all concern for everything else. Tomorrow didn't matter. Nothing mattered but the terrible need that only he could satisfy.

"God, Melinda!" He threw his full weight upon her and she welcomed it gladly, joyously. His lips met hers at the same moment as they became fully one and she moaned as she felt the fulfillment of their joining.

His movements were slow, almost languid, and she looked up at him through heavy-lidded eyes.

"I want it to last," he said thickly. "To last a long time."

She could not respond with words; her breath came too rapidly for coherent speech, but her hips arched up, automatically seeking contact with him, and her fingers dug into his back. She, too, wanted it to last.

But the sweetness was almost unbearable, the pleasure close to pain. Her body writhed beneath his, caught in the throes of a passion from which there was only one escape—the final consummation.

Higher and higher he drove her eager body until she

fell over the cliff in a crashing sweep of ecstasy. Only moments later she heard his own sounds of fulfillment. But by that time she had come to rest, like a swimmer floating in a warm pool of contentment.

For long moments he remained inert upon her, the weight of his body a welcome thing. When he did roll over, he drew her with him. Not letting their flesh separate for even a moment, he kept her body close against his side.

Melinda was suddenly very tired, it was a sweet exhaustion—soft and warm—and she lay against him in complete and mindless relaxation.

"Go to sleep now," he murmured softly, his hand stroking her hair gently.

She wanted to protest that the night was still young, that there were many hours left, hours too precious to waste in slumber, but her tongue was too heavy to move and she drifted off, to dream pleasantly of lying safe in Cal's arms.

12

The night was far from wasted, however, for periodically she awoke to find Cal reaching for her again. And she surrendered herself fully to him, awaking in the early morning with such a feeling of contentment that she could not keep herself from smiling.

"You look like the cat that swallowed the canary," he said, glancing down at her with a grin.

Melinda stretched luxuriously. "I feel like it," she admitted, still half-asleep.

"You shouldn't do that," he said, his eyes gleaming as he moved toward her. "I was going to take you for another ride, but now—"

They had their ride, though its beginning was somewhat delayed. Through the whole morning Melinda felt like two people. One was a young woman joyful and radiant, glorying in the sheer pleasure of her experience, not caring for anything beyond the present moment. The other, dour-faced and bitter, kept reminding her that tomorrow would come and then she would be sorry.

When they returned to the ranch, the sun was high in the sky. Melinda was still managing to keep the doomsayer at bay. She smiled as Cal's hands encircled her waist and lifted her easily to the ground. And she moved quite readily into his arms for his kiss. It was not the brief kiss she had expected and she felt her blood begin to heat.

"How about a little nap?" he said, his dark eyes teasing. "You didn't get much sleep last night."

"Would I get any now?" she asked, her eyes wide with innocence.

Cal chuckled. "'Fraid not." He held her even tighter. "You do things to me, woman."

She felt her body against the tenseness of his and knew that she desired him again. "Let's go inside," she whispered, wondering at her own daring.

He had hurried her across the yard and into the house and was pulling her through the library when the phone shrilled. "Damn!" He eyed the phone savagely, almost as though it were an enemy.

"You'd better answer it," Melinda said reasonably. "It might be important."

The phone rang again and with a muttered curse he scooped it up. "Hello!"

His hand had not released hers and she stood looking up into his face. His features hardened before her very eyes. "Nicole! I told you—"

Melinda's heart rushed up into her throat and she tried to extricate her fingers from his, but he merely tightened his grip.

"Nicole! You can't!"

For a long moment he stood silent, the muscles in his jaw standing out as he fought for control. Finally he laid the phone back in its cradle with a care that indicated more surely than words the fierceness of the rage rushing through him.

Yet when he turned to her, his tone was even. "That was Nicole. She'll be here in five minutes."

Melinda tried to keep her expression blank but she knew she was unsuccessful from the look on his face. "I tried to tell her not to come, but she didn't give me a chance," he said. "I'll get rid of her, though. Inside of ten minutes she'll be gone."

Reality came rushing back on Melinda in cold icy waves. Here she was, alone with Colin Marsden, about to face his irate almost-fiancée. In the past hours she had not once thought of Nicole. A grave mistake, for Nicole fought for what she considered hers. Melinda could hardly blame her for that. What woman wouldn't want a husband like Cal?

"Do you want me to wait in the other room?" she asked as his fingers finally released hers and they moved out into the living room. In spite of her efforts, her voice did not reflect firm acceptance of the situation.

"Of course not."

She saw that his anger had not faded; it was still there, though curbed. "I just thought—" she began.

"Well, don't." He glared at her. "Nicole doesn't run my life. I go where I please, with whom I pl—"

There was the sharp staccato of heels on the porch and the front door closed with a bang behind an irate Nicole Erin. She was not dressed for a drive through hot dusty country and she looked warm and disheveled.

"Hello, Nicole." His voice carried warning.

"Hello, Miss Erin." Melinda thought she might as well follow his lead.

"Hello." Nicole's eyes shot daggers though her tone was even.

"I'm sorry you drove all this way for nothing," Cal said. "As you can see, I'm busy."

"I need to talk to you now." Nicole's tone brooked no interference. "It's very impor—"

The shrill ring of the phone interrupted this and with a

worried look at the two women Cal moved into the library to answer it.

He did not close the door behind him, Melinda noticed, almost as though he feared what the women might do to each other. Nicole moved closer, but Melinda held her ground.

"I guess you didn't pay much attention to me the other day," Nicole began, in what was obviously intended to resemble a friendly tone. "But I really think you should consider my advice. Colin is way out of your class, you know." In spite of her feigned friendliness she could not keep her contempt out of her eyes. "I know that he amuses himself with other women." She smiled smugly. "That doesn't bother me. After all, men will be men. And that's all you are to him—an amusement. Our marriage is arranged." Nicole's eyes narrowed shrewdly. "You really shouldn't waste your time, my dear. Colin would never marry so far beneath him."

Melinda had intended to keep her anger well under control, but at the mention of their already arranged marriage her blood began to boil. Still, she did not want to let herself go. It was demeaning to let someone like Nicole Erin get to her.

Therefore she kept her features expressionless and her voice calm as she replied. "I'm sure your advice is well-intentioned, Miss Erin, but it is you who are wasting your time. Marriage is the furthest thing from my thoughts. Indeed, I'm sorry you had to go to so much trouble for no good reason. To drive all the way out here and get yourself in such a state."

She could not refrain from that one little jab, she thought as she noticed Nicole wince. How dreadful to have to look absolutely perfect at every moment. How did Nicole manage that in bed? But the thought and the pictures it presented to her mind were too painful to pursue. Instead she focused all her attention on remaining calm and cool.

Nicole looked about to say something else spiteful, but just then Cal returned to the room. He cast Melinda a worried look. "I'll just walk Nicole out to her car," he said, his fingers already under the other woman's elbow. "I won't be long."

"Take all the time you want." Melinda hoped the words sounded as sweet as she meant them to. It was only by great effort that she refrained from adding the word darling. There wasn't much use in enraging Nicole further.

As the front door closed behind the two, Melinda began to tremble. She could not go on like this, she told herself. She should never have come here. Blindly she headed up the stairs toward the bedroom.

Five minutes later when Cal found her there, she had the suitcase neatly packed. She rose with it as he entered the room. "I want to go back to Helena," she said, her voice as firm as she could make it.

"We will. Later." His dark eyes were cloudy with worry.

"I want to go now."

He shook his head. "It's too early. We've got a couple hours yet."

"I want to go now," she repeated stubbornly. She considered trying to go around him, but he leaned nonchalantly against the frame, filling the doorway.

"You want to use 'When Branding Comes Round' on the cover of your book, don't you?"

She almost dropped the suitcase in her surprise. "What has that to do with anything?" she demanded angrily.

"You have to have my permission to reproduce it. You know that."

Her anger grew then and she let the suitcase hit the floor with a bang. "Listen to me, Colin Marsden. I don't give a damn about your picture!" That was not the truth, of course, but she was so angry she didn't care. "You can take your painting and go to hell!"

"You left all your notes in the gallery," he reminded her, and now his eyes began to gleam with that look she knew so well. He was enjoying her anger! As though to verify this, he let his eyes slide over her and she grew extremely conscious of the heaving of her breasts beneath the thin cotton shirt. "You're very attractive when you're angry, Melinda. Very attractive." He straightened slowly and moved toward her.

"Cal!" She put her hands up instinctively. "No! Don't!"

He was only a few inches away. "Don't what?" he said softly, letting his eyes caress her face.

"Don't—look at me like that!" Her voice had lost some of its firmness and trembled slightly.

"Why?" The single word was fraught with emotion and he took the final step between them.

"I—" She faltered and could not go on. With him standing so close to her, with him eyeing her in that hungry way, her body had begun to respond to his.

"I don't like it," she said, her voice falling away to a whisper.

"You don't like it or you like it too much?" he asked as his hands settled on her waist.

"I—I don't have to answer that," she said finally. "You're—not being fair."

His laugh caught her by surprise. "Melinda, my silly. All's fair in love and war."

This is not love! She wanted to scream it at him, but before the words could leave her mouth he had pulled her against him and his lips covered hers. It was a long kiss and deliberately sensuous. He remembered what

174

had worked with her before and he expertly coaxed out of her the response he wanted, his hands moving over her back, her hips, molding her softness against him. She felt his urgent need and her own boiled inside her, but still she struggled to retain her sanity.

Finally he succeeded in teasing her mouth open and his tongue mingled with hers. At the same time one hand slid up to caress the sensitive nape of her neck and Melinda knew there was no sense fighting it any longer. He would get his way; he would have her one more time. And then it would all be over.

She wanted to cry out, to stop him from taking her body this last time, for she knew deeply and innately that every time they joined she became more enmeshed with him; he became more necessary to her existence. It was this, she realized suddenly, that sparked so much of her anger with him. The intimacies they shared took her further and further into a union with him that was far more than physical. But that was not the case for him. He saw each event as a whole in itself, not as part of a process that forged ever stronger bonds between a man and a woman.

She could not stop him now. Her body was as avid as his for their approaching union. And, in spite of her instinctive recognition that the greater her joy now the greater her pain tomorrow, she could hold nothing of herself back, reacting to his kisses and caresses with every cell in her body, kissing and caressing in her turn.

When finally he completed their union, she could only cling to him convulsively, her cries mingling with his hoarse moans until he drove them both over the top into ecstasy.

As before, he left his weight on her for some time. She clung to him as her breathing slowed, fighting the lump of tears that rose in her throat, wishing there were some way, any way, to bind him to her irrevocably, as irrevocably as she already felt bound to him. But she knew there was no way. This man could not be bound.

And he was a good man. She knew that. He gave much more of himself than Tom Ryder ever had. It was that that made him so devastating, she thought, swallowing hard over the lump in her throat. She could not imagine him ever being happy with Nicole Erin. The woman's shallow nature was far too apparent.

He rolled onto his back, taking her with him, keeping her body close against his side. "I feel better now," he said softly, his fingers making lazy circles on her back. "How about you?"

She sighed. In spite of the warnings of her brain, she felt very good. He had satisfied her body in a way no man ever had. It was not his fault that in some indefinable way he had also satisfied her soul, and that the memory of that double satisfaction would poison any future relationships for her. "Me, too."

"Good." The arm around her tightened. "In a little while we'll head back for Helena. Okay?"

"Okay."

The ride back seemed very short to Melinda, knowing what she did about her feelings for this man. She tried not to get caught taking little sidelong glances at him, but she wanted to imprint his features on her memory.

The car pulled into the motel parking lot long before she was ready for it. Cal pulled her toward him for a swift kiss. "I'll see you tomorrow," he said with a smile. "I'll have something special to give you then." His fingers caressed her cheek. Then he was out of the car and opening her door. He put the suitcase in her numbed hand, gave her a peck on the forehead, jumped back in the car and drove off.

For long minutes Melinda stood there, fighting the tears that welled up in her eyes. Tomorrow at lunch he would give her the permission papers and that would be the end of it. She bit her bottom lip to keep from screaming out in her hurt and rage. What a fool she had been. She would not be able to work in the gallery now; she saw that clearly. To be in his presence, or even just his house, and know it was over would be more than she could bear.

Tomorrow, after she got the coveted permission papers, she would pack up her notes and leave. Even if he wanted to see her again, she could not do it. For her own protection she must stop this thing now. Before she was irretrievably lost. If she wasn't already.

13

⁂

Melinda parked the red Camaro outside the Marsden Mansion at 11:45 the next morning. She had not been able to bring herself to get there any earlier. In fact, if she hadn't left all her notes there, she probably wouldn't have gone at all. Permission papers could be mailed, after all.

She glanced down once at her casual jeans and boots and sighed. She hadn't had the energy to dress up. And anyway she would be leaving immediately. She would take her papers and head for Havre and the old ranch. Surely the people who lived there wouldn't object to her taking a look around.

Carruthers's smile was warm as he opened the door. At first she thought he was going to say something to her, but when he remained silent, she decided she'd been wrong.

Her heart beat faster and faster as the elevator neared the third floor and she thought surely Cal would be able to hear it from the other room. She crossed to the gallery door with hesitation and then, taking a deep breath, turned the knob.

Jim Pederson looked up from his desk, then got hurriedly to his feet. "Melinda! It's good to see you!"

"Hello, Jim." She knew she sounded distracted, but she couldn't help it. "I was supposed to meet—"

"Yes, I know." His hand under her elbow guided her toward the table. "Mr. Marsden will be late. He asked me to tell you so. You'll be glad to know that he's given you blanket permission. You can use any painting in the gallery." He shook his head slightly as though bemused. "Even 'When Branding Comes Round.' I don't know how you did it."

Melinda's nails dug into her palms in her effort to still her trembling. "Where is—Mr. Marsden?"

Jim Pederson's nose wrinkled fastidiously. "He had an urgent call from Miss Erin."

"I see." She had to turn away to keep from revealing her emotions. Quickly she walked toward the far corner of the room and began to gather her papers. With great effort she kept herself from stuffing them madly in her briefcase. She would work calmly but swiftly.

A few minutes later, clutching the briefcase, she turned back toward Pederson, who was watching her with curious eyes. "Where are the permission papers?" she asked.

"There. On the desk."

Melinda reached for them.

"But he wants you to wait," Pederson said. "He'll be here as soon as he can. Cook is holding lunch."

"Tell Mr. Marsden, thank you," she replied stiffly. "I appreciate the papers. Unfortuantely I can't wait for lunch. Good-bye."

"But Melinda—"

The tears were so close that further speech was impossible and she hurried into the little elevator. As it slowly made its way downward she used every trick she knew to keep the tears at bay.

Carruthers was not in the lower hall and she hurried out, her boot heels clomping on the highly polished wooden floor. Reaching the red Camaro, she still dared not give way. Cal might come back at any moment and she simply could not face him. She might break then, might let the man see the strength of her feelings for him, this insane desire to belong to him totally. And she couldn't do that. She had no right. It was Nicole Erin who would take that place in his life. Right this minute he was with her. Melinda bit her lip at the thought.

Then, straightening her shoulders, she reached for the ignition. She would just hold these feelings, she told herself, until she reached the ranch in Havre. Out on the prairie, away from everyone, then she could give her feelings full rein. Until then she would be a practical, reasonable person, her mind on the road or on her work.

Some hours later Melinda stopped the car at the end of a rutted lane and stared in disbelief. The old ranch house was deserted. No chickens scratched in the yard. No cattle fed on the adjacent prairie. Tumbleweeds lay, caught by the porch railing, and sagebrush had invaded the yard. Part of the stable roof had caved in, leaving a gaping hole. There was not a sign of life anywhere.

Over the years Melinda had thought often of Gramps and the ranch, but she had never considered finding it like this.

She climbed out of the Camaro and approached the house. The steps, though they were still sound, creaked under her boots as she climbed up to the veranda and moved across it to the door. Her hand rested on the knob for long moments before she tentatively turned it and felt it open in her hands. For several minutes she hesitated, then with a sigh she pushed the door open.

The little living room was bare and dusty, festooned

with spider webs. A battered rocker, some of its dowels missing, sat alone in the middle of the floor. In a daze, Melinda crossed to it and sat down.

Then the tears came. She cried for long minutes, great jerking sobs for the days that were gone, the love that was lost.

The West had been very cruel to her, she thought, as sometime later she still sat there, now dry-eyed, the old rocker moving gently. The West had offered her love—not once, but twice—and then snatched it away.

She could work through her grief about Gramps. His love would be always with her, a kind of hidden strength that was a legacy from him. It was good to have.

Her love for Cal was different. Memories of him were too wrenching to give her strength. Thinking of him, of his smile, of his long lean body, the feel of him against her, would only cause her pain—almost unbearable pain.

The West was not what it had been. The past was irrevocably gone. There were no more men like Gramps had told her about, no more men like Gramps himself. She sighed there in the gathering dusk. For a while it had seemed to her that Cal might be such a man—a real man in touch with the land. And perhaps he even was. But like the old-time cowboy he could not be corralled. He would light here—or there—but only for a spell. And then he would be off somewhere else.

Slowly she let her eyes fall shut. Maybe she could recapture a little of Gramps' spirit here in the place where he had given her so much. Draw from her memories of him the strength to carry on. For his sake she must finish the Russell book. It had no special purpose for her now. Tenure and teaching both seemed equally unreal to her. But she would have to carry on. She was far too healthy to die of a broken heart and the rest of her life must have some center to it.

She let herself slide back into the past, the memories of Gramps' stories, the warmth of his raspy voice, gradually shutting out everything around her.

It was some time later and she had almost succeeded in obliterating the present when the sound of an approaching motor brought her swiftly back. In one startled movement she was on her feet and at the dirty window. A car was coming up the lane, Cal's battered station wagon.

Panic assailed Melinda. She could not face him now. God knows what terrible things she might say, what a fool she might make of herself. She crossed the room and slipped through the little kitchen and out the back door. Trying to keep the house between the car and her retreating figure, she broke into a run. If he didn't see her, if she could get far enough away to hide, he might never find her. The waiting rented car, the well-known fact of his persistence, meant nothing to her. Running clumsily, the boots hampering her awkward progress, she knew only that she had to get away. To have him touch her again would be unbearable.

She heard no sound behind her, but her heart was pounding so loudly in her ears that nothing else was audible. She must get away, she told herself. She must. And then the tears began to fall again. They streamed down her cheeks in torrents, blinding her and making her flight over the uneven ground even more difficult. But still she pushed on.

It was a prairie dog hole that stopped her finally, catching her boot and throwing her to the ground with a force that knocked the breath from her. She lay there for a moment, her lungs gasping for air.

And then she saw Cal. He was almost upon her. Although he was walking, he had evidently just slowed his pace, for his chest heaved with the effort of his breathing. She struggled to her knees.

"Melinda! Wait!"

It was not his words that held her, though, but the hard weight of his body as he flung himself at her

She fought him with all the strength she had, knowing only that if he took her again in that loveless way she would want to die. But she could not win against him. He pinned her to the prairie grass with his lean hard body and waited until she was too exhausted to fight any longer.

She stared up at him, her eyes brimming with tears. "Please," she begged, desperation cracking her voice. "Please let me go."

He did not answer, only staring down at her with an intensity that finally caused her to close her eyes.

And then his lips met hers. She tried again to escape him, her agonized mind screaming with the humiliation of being used so callously by the man she loved. But she could not stop the traitorous reaction of her body. It belonged to him completely.

The kiss was not long, but it left her weak and helpless beneath him. "Now," he said firmly. "I want some answers. And I'm going to get them. Why did you run away from me?"

She summoned all her anger, hoping rage would serve her where reason did not. "I won't allow you to treat me this way." She wanted to scream it at him, but her voice cracked. "You can marry Nicole. Have all the playmates you like. Except—me. You'll never have me!"

His answer was another kiss, one that left her even weaker than the first. "Listen," he said, his face only inches from hers. "I'm not looking for a playmate. In Deadwood, when I approached you like I did—I'd never done that before."

Her eyes mirrored her disbelief.

"Give me credit for some sense, Melinda. I haven't had the bushels of women you seem to think I have. For one

183

thing it's too dangerous for a man in my position—paternity suits can be very dirty. And with women throwing themselves at me—or my money—I just soured on the whole thing."

"Nicole—"

He shook his head. "I should have known she had something to do with this." He eyed her shrewdly. "She's the one who told you I played around, isn't she?"

Melinda did not deny it. She stared up into the dark face so near her own, hardly able to believe what she was hearing.

"Our supposed marriage was Nicole's idea," Cal went on. "Not mine. I guess she thought she'd wear me down eventually. But I knew I'd never marry her."

"Then why—"

"Why did I let her hang around?"

Melinda nodded.

"Think," he said. "She offered me an easy out. Kept a lot of women away from me." His dark eyes grew warm. "I never proposed to Nicole. I never asked her to be my wife—to share my life."

All the breath was gone from Melinda's body. She stared at him, mesmerized.

"I'm asking you, Melinda. Will you marry me?"

"But this morning— You were with her."

"I couldn't propose to you until I had convinced her we were not going to be a couple." He sighed. "She got hysterical and threw a tantrum. By the time I got her calmed down, you were gone." He kissed the tip of her nose. "Didn't Pederson tell you I was coming?"

"Yes, but—" She couldn't go on.

"You haven't said yes." His glance was worried. "I know we didn't get off to such a great start, but I hoped I'd remedied that." His forehead puckered into a frown. "For God's sake, Melinda, answer me!"

She tried to gather her scattered wits. "I—I can hardly

think. I'm a teacher, Cal. Not a socialite. I need to be myself. And there's the book."

He smiled. "I don't want a socialite. And as for teaching, there are schools in Montana, you know. Of course you'll finish the book. We owe Russell that. He brought us together. But listen, haven't you wanted to paint?"

"Of course. And I have. But the West haunted my imagination, the old West in all its glory. And I could never be as good as Russell, as those who lived here then."

Cal pretended to frown. "What's wrong with the new West? The West you and I can help build. Your brush can record that."

Looking up, Melinda grew serious. "I'll marry you on one condition."

Concern returned to his eyes and she felt his body stiffen in apprehension. "Name it."

"You have to paint, too," she said softly. "Otherwise it's no deal."

She felt his sigh of relief, then his lips were nuzzling her ear. "You drive a hard bargain, woman," he said.

Melinda smiled. "I love you," she said. "Give me an answer, Cal. Give me your word you'll paint, too."

There was a moment's hesitation and then he whispered, "All right, my love. You have my word." He planted another kiss on her nose and one on each eyelid before he rose to his feet, extending a hand to help her. "We'd better get back to the ranch. It's going to be dark soon."

Arms around each other's waists, they turned back toward the ramshackle ranch house. "I have an engagement ring for you," he said as he matched his stride to her shorter one. "It's very old and belonged to my mother."

"Oh, Cal, how lovely!"

He smiled ruefully. "It's still in the gallery. I meant to give it to you at lunch. When I heard you were gone, I couldn't think of anything but finding you. Thank God, I knew about this ranch."

She tightened the arm around him. "I don't need a ring," she said, pride in her voice. "I know I belong to you."

His smile grew thoughtful. "I have a great idea for an engagement present."

"Cal, I don't need—"

"Oh, you'll love this one. We'll buy this place and restore it. We can use it weekends—when we don't want anyone to find us."

Melinda turned sparkling eyes to his. "We can fill it with our paintings," she cried.

He grinned. "Can't we have just a few Russells?" he asked plaintively.

Melinda's laughter rang out across the darkening prairie. "I guess we can have a few if you promise not to let them put you off your work."

He swung her around to face him, his dark eyes greedily devouring her flushed face. "I'll promise if you will," he replied.

Melinda's nod was triumphant and her hand reached out automatically to caress the strong line of his chin. "It's a bargain then."

His grin was wide. "You know how bargains are best sealed, don't you?"

"No." Her eyes were mischievous.

"Then I'll show you." And he swept her into his arms and covered her lips with his own. And there, under the darkening prairie sky, she returned his kiss with all her pent-up longing. Her heart soared with the joy of it. For now they were to be truly joined—the union that she had so desired and never imagined possible would become a reality. A beautiful, loving, lasting reality.

YOU'LL BE SWEPT AWAY
WITH SILHOUETTE DESIRE

$1.75 each

1 ☐ CORPORATE AFFAIR
James

2 ☐ LOVE'S SILVER WEB
Monet

3 ☐ WISE FOLLY
Clay

4 ☐ KISS AND TELL
Carey

5 ☐ WHEN LAST WE LOVED
Baker

6 ☐ A FRENCHMAN'S KISS
Mallory

7 ☐ NOT EVEN FOR LOVE
St. Claire

8 ☐ MAKE NO PROMISES
Dee

9 ☐ MOMENT IN TIME
Simms

10 ☐ WHENEVER I LOVE YOU
Smith

$1.95 each

11 ☐ VELVET TOUCH
James

12 ☐ THE COWBOY AND THE
LADY   Palmer

13 ☐ COME BACK, MY LOVE
Wallace

14 ☐ BLANKET OF STARS
Valley

15 ☐ SWEET BONDAGE
Vernon

16 ☐ DREAM COME TRUE
Major

17 ☐ OF PASSION BORN
Simms

18 ☐ SECOND HARVEST
Ross

19 ☐ LOVER IN PURSUIT
James

20 ☐ KING OF DIAMONDS
Allison

21 ☐ LOVE INTHE CHINA SEA
Baker

22 ☐ BITTERSWEET IN BERN
Durant

23 ☐ CONSTANT STRANGER
Sunshine

24 ☐ SHARED MOMENTS
Baxter

25 ☐ RENAISSANCE MAN
James

26 ☐ SEPTEMBER MORNING
Palmer

27 ☐ ON WINGS OF NIGHT
Conrad

28 ☐ PASSIONATE JOURNEY
Lovan

29 ☐ ENCHANTED DESERT
Michelle

30 ☐ PAST FORGETTING
Lind

31 ☐ RECKLESS PASSION
James

32 ☐ YESTERDAY'S DREAMS
Clay

Silhouette Desire

Coming Next Month

Affair Of Honor by Stephanie James

When Ryder Sterne held her in his embrace, Philosophy professor Brenna Llewellyn almost forgot why she was at the mountain retreat, and soon found herself abandoning all logic for love.

Friends And Lovers by Diana Palmer

They were close friends, but now Madeline found that John's touch was somehow different. It ignited a passion in her that led them to discover a whole new closeness.

Shadow Of The Mountain by Pamela Lind

Deke Jordan had rights and could lay equal claim to Shelley Grant's small mining company. But Shelley didn't expect him to stake a claim on her with kisses she fought—but couldn't resist.

Embers Of The Sun by Raye Morgan

Artist Charla Evans came to Japan to study raku pottery—and to escape an unhappy love. But then she met tycoon Stephen Conners and realized she couldn't live for art alone!

Winter Lady by Janet Joyce

America's heartthrob Devlin Paige saved Raine Morgan when he rescued her on the ski slopes in Minnesota's desolate hills . . . but he left Raine burning with a reckless passion she couldn't escape.

If Ever You Need Me by Paula Fulford

When Julia Somers stepped off the stage in triumph, producer Roy Allison offered her a star-making role . . . and more. But could love be real in his celluloid world?

Get 6 new Silhouette Special Editions every month for a 15–day FREE trial!

Free Home Delivery, Free Previews, Free Bonus Books. Silhouette Special Editions are a new kind of romance novel. These are big, powerful stories that will capture your imagination. They're longer, with fully developed characters and intricate plots that will hold you spellbound from the first page to the very last.

Each month we will send you six exciting *new* Silhouette Special Editions, just as soon as they are published. If you enjoy them as much as we think you will, pay the invoice enclosed with your shipment. **They're delivered right to your door with never a charge for postage or handling, and there's no obligation to buy anything at any time.** To start receiving Silhouette Special Editions regularly, mail the coupon below today.

Silhouette Special Edition

READERS' COMMENTS ON SILHOUETTE DESIRES

"Thank you for Silhouette Desires. They are the best thing that has happened to the bookshelves in a long time."
—V.W.*, Knoxville, TN

"Silhouette Desires—wonderful, fantastic—the best romance around."
—H.T.*, Margate, N.J.

"As a writer as well as a reader of romantic fiction, I found DESIREs most refreshingly realistic—and definitely as magical as the love captured on their pages."
—C.M.*, Silver Lake, N.Y.

*names available on request